PENGUIN  CLASSICS

KALLOCAIN

KARIN BOYE (1900–41) was born in Gothenburg, Sweden and studied in Stockholm and Uppsala. As a young woman she joined the international socialist and pacifist organization Clarté and published her first volume of poetry while still in her early twenties. She translated T. S. Eliot's *The Waste Land* into Swedish in 1931, and wrote several novels throughout the decade. She married a fellow writer but left her husband after undergoing psychoanalysis in Berlin and formed a lifelong relationship with a German woman, Margot Hanel. Boye's most famous book, *Kallocain* (1940), was partly inspired by eye-opening trips to Nazi Germany and Soviet Russia. She died from an overdose of sleeping pills the year after writing the novel.

DAVID MCDUFF's translations for Penguin Classics include Dostoyevsky's *Crime and Punishment, The Brothers Karamazov* and *The Idiot*, and Babel's short stories.

KARIN BOYE

Kallocain

A novel from the 21st century

Translated and with an Introduction by
DAVID MCDUFF

PENGUIN BOOKS

PENGUIN CLASSICS

UK | USA | Canada | Ireland | Australia
India | New Zealand | South Africa

Penguin Books is part of the Penguin Random House group of companies
whose addresses can be found at global.penguinrandomhouse.com.

First published in in Stockholm by Albert Bonniers Boktryckeri in 1940
This edition published in Penguin Classics 2019

002

Translation and introduction copyright © David McDuff, 2019
The moral right of the translator has been asserted

Set in 10.25/12.25pt Sabon LT Std
Typeset by Jouve (UK), Milton Keynes
Printed and bound in Great Britain by Clays Ltd, Elcograf S.p.A.

The authorized representative in the EEA is Penguin Random House Ireland,
Morrison Chambers, 32 Nassau Street, Dublin DO2 YH68

A CIP catalogue record for this book is available from the British Library

ISBN: 978-0-241-60830-2

www.greenpenguin.co.uk

MIX
Paper from
responsible sources
FSC® C018179

Penguin Random House is committed to a
sustainable future for our business, our readers
and our planet. This book is made from Forest
Stewardship Council® certified paper.

Contents

Introduction

'I'm scared,' the Swedish poet, novelist and essayist Karin Boye told her friend, the writer Harry Martinson, when they discussed her acclaimed novel *Kallocain* (1940) on their last meeting. Her mother, after reading the book, told her that she had 'done it well'. 'Do you think *I* did it?' was the reply.[1]

The author's fear was partly related to the political context: she was concerned that her book might draw the attention of neutral Sweden's security police, who were on watch for signs of anything that might spark an invasion by Nazi Germany. She even considered revising the work and giving all of its characters Chinese names (which only a few characters in the published version have), in the hope that this would have the effect of 'neutralizing' the text. Fortunately, the danger was avoided, and the book passed almost unnoticed by the Swedish authorities. Nonetheless, in early 1940, ordinary Swedish citizens had to be careful whom they talked to and what they talked about – even what books they bought and read. Authors had to be even more careful with what they released in print.

Boye's sense of disquiet also reflected the mystery of how she had managed to write a science-fiction novel that was unlike anything she had produced before, and unlike almost anything that had appeared in earlier Swedish literature. Somehow, the war that was engulfing Europe had triggered something within her that made it possible for her to create a vision of enslaved humanity, an allegory dream-like and grotesque, yet instantly recognizable to anyone then living through the international crisis.

Kallocain was the last major work of Karin Boye, who was

born in 1900 and wrote during the 1920s and 1930s. In those decades the 'ice-cold reasoning' of Hitler and the 'merciless dialectics' of Stalin began to dominate the political and intellectual scene, and the novel was among the international reactions of horror at what was taking place in Europe. On the book's first publication, it attracted strongly positive reviews. The modernist poet Artur Lundkvist called it 'in the international class', while others characterized it as 'a work of art', with one critic suggesting that in her novel she had injected a dose of the truth drug Kallocain into the world of 1940 and 'enabled it to lay bare its innermost tendencies'.[2]

Boye's early writing had been subjective in character: for the most part, meditative poetry that reflected on an inward journey towards God or individual personal fulfilment and transformation. Partly as a result of economic pressure, she began to write fiction and reviews for literary journals. She also made literary translations, including Thomas Mann's *The Magic Mountain* (1924), a work she later criticized for its male-centredness, and the socialist realist novel *Cement* (1925) by the Soviet author Fyodor Gladkov, which she translated from German, a language she mastered with almost native fluency and spoke with only a slight Swedish accent. At the same time, she became involved in the socialist politics of the Stockholm Clarté group, whose members included the poet Gunnar Ekelöf and the author, critic and translator Erik Mesterton, and in 1928, together with some of them, she made a study visit to the Soviet Union. After this visit, which seems to have consisted mainly in a drab pilgrimage between various state institutions, factories and collective farms, she became disillusioned with Soviet life and politics.

Gradually, she moved away from the group's aims and outlook, and concentrated on writing and publishing a series of novels, as well as several collections of poetry. With Mesterton, she edited the avant-garde literary magazine *Spektrum*, which drew its inspiration from French Surrealism, the Imagism of T. S. Eliot and Ezra Pound and also literary Freudianism. With Mesterton's help, she translated Eliot's *The Waste Land*, and then made her first experiments in psychoanalysis (which continued until her death), which were connected with her desire to confront her own homosexual and bisexual identity in terms that might make her free and independent. The analysis was mostly conducted in Berlin, under professional medical guidance, and led to her ending her heterosexual marriage and embarking on a relationship with a young German-Jewish woman, Margot Hanel, with whom she lived, more or less, until the end of her life.

During her visits to Berlin in the early 1930s, Boye witnessed the rise of Nazism at first hand. On one occasion, together with the critic Vilhelm Scharp, she attended a large election rally at the Sportpalast, where Hermann Goering delivered a speech filled with demagogic rhetoric. According to her biographer Margit Abenius:

> Scharp observed Karin, who stood with her arm stretched aloft, making the Hitler salute, seemingly in complete fascination. Not to make that gesture could cost one's life – neither more nor less.[3]

All of these experiences flowed together in the writing of *Kallocain*, which she seems to have begun in the late autumn of 1939. 'Yes, these have been strange times,' she wrote to a Norwegian colleague in the spring of 1940, in the context of the German invasion and occupation of Norway, '– the political passions have turned old friends into enemies and caused nervous crises in young people . . .' She mentioned a 'low point' tempered by 'the awareness that the values we possess – between one another – are the most precious of all and the most easily lost'. It was in this context that she created her dystopian novel, in which she portrayed not only earth-shaking world events, but also their destructive effects on individual human beings.

In Europe and America the dystopian novel had established itself as a literary genre in the early twentieth century. Although the antecedents of the genre include the prophetic and speculative writings of nineteenth-century authors like Jules Verne (*Paris in the Twentieth Century*) and Imre Madách (*The Tragedy of Man*), the political and theological parable of the Grand Inquisitor in Fyodor Dostoyevsky's novel *The Brothers Karamazov*, and the futuristic fantasies of H. G. Wells (*The Time Machine*, *The War of the Worlds*, *The First Men on the Moon*), it was not until the publication in 1924 of an English translation of the novel *We* by the Soviet author Yevgeny Zamyatin that the genre emerged in its modern form, as exemplified also by works like Aldous Huxley's *Brave New World* (1932), Sinclair Lewis's *It Can't Happen Here* (1935), George Orwell's *1984* (1949), and Ray Bradbury's *Fahrenheit 451* (1953).

The critic Erika Gottlieb has characterized dystopian fiction (the term dates from the early 1950s) as 'a post-Christian genre',[4] meaning by this that in dystopian works the historical religious conflict between divine salvation and damnation has been replaced by a secular clash; between a vision of enlightened leadership in the service of social justice and a nightmare of dictatorship and political and personal repression. Although it is not mentioned in Gottlieb's study, *Kallocain* displays nearly all the characteristic features of the dystopian genre. Particularly, in Gottlieb's terms, it shows 'the protagonist [of] an ultimate trial' in confrontation with the 'Grand Inquisitor' of secular, totalitarian authority, and also obliquely expresses the fear that Western intellectuals are too ready to condone the Soviet and Nazi dictatorships, unwilling to admit that the Soviet state is founded on terror, just like its alleged opponent, Nazism.

Subtitled 'A novel from the 21st century', like other books in the genre it depicts a totalitarian future that is really a warning about the dangers of the present day – in the case of *Kallocain*, the Second World War. In 1939 the accommodation between Germany and the Soviet Union, known as the Nazi-Soviet Pact, was signed by Ribbentrop and Molotov, and for the next two years the Nazi leadership worked hand in hand with the Soviet government, dividing and invading Poland, and forming an anti-Western alliance headed by Hitler and Stalin. *Kallocain*'s mechanized, dehumanized landscape is a composite, bearing the traits of both Nazi and Soviet society: here elements of racial biology co-exist with rigid class distinctions, both equally aimed at wiping out the individual conscience and consciousness. Karin Boye had read the work of both Zamyatin and Huxley, and her multi-ethnic totalitarian World State displays elements familiar from *We* and *Brave New World* – but her narrative has an urgency that is connected with a new and specific historical juncture: the outbreak of the Second World War, and a reality that looks both unpredictable and frightening.

In his essay about the novel, Ekelöf later described the general mood of the time:

> Karin Boye's *Kallocain* appeared in 1940, in perhaps the darkest autumn of the democracies, a disastrous year for such a book. Spain had formed the run-up to the long series of political and military depredations, the Battle of Britain was on, the war in Greece was beginning. On every other street corner glowed the shameless orange posters, and people preferred to avoid listening to German radio. Many were getting used to the idea that there would be no future except underground.[5]

The novel's tone and diction mirror the creeping process of alienation it describes: much of Leo Kall's first-person narrative is written in a detached, unemotional style that sometimes recalls the narratives of Kafka. The secret memoir of a committed bureaucrat and government scientist, it maintains an impersonal aloofness (*kall* is the Swedish adjective for 'cold', 'callous') that is broken only occasionally by scenes and details that suggest the existence of another life below the surface, where human beings actually live, love and suffer. In the bleak, Dantesque landscape of the novel Boye creates a world that is described in meticulous detail. We see 'police eyes' and 'police ears' – cameras and microphones – in the walls of houses and apartments, the card-index systems of the police and intelligence services, the interior of an aircraft, a commune of dissidents and resisters, a state-run dining room. The plot is driven by the story of the 'truth drug', Kallocain, that Kall has developed, which probably has its origins in press coverage of the 1937 Moscow show trials, where the confessions of the 'Trotskyists' and 'Right Oppositionists' were said to have been induced by drugs (scopolamine, the 'truth serum', was often mentioned) or torture. But the core of the narrative lies in the tension between repression and expression, inner and outer, constriction and freedom. 'You have broken me open like a tin can, by force,' Kall's wife Linda tells him, echoing the author's own assertion in a letter to an acquaintance that 'all human beings want to be forced open like tin cans, *want* to open themselves.' Reor, the 'great man' who is the subject of a myth that sustains the community of dissidents and outcasts living under the surface of the World State, exists in their memory as a Christ-like figure, the centre of something that resembles a religion, suppressed and persecuted by the authorities. He is a symbol of openness and freedom, suspended in time and opposed to the hard, metallic armour of the state.

Kallocain reflects a world in which no one can be trusted – with the collapse of democracy, all are at the mercy of two states, two totalitarian value and belief systems that threaten to crush the individual and obliterate him or her entirely. Because of the absence of trust, no succour is to be found in human relationships, in friendship or in marriage: with the implementation of new thought-crime laws enabled by his drug, Kall anticipates 'colleagues denouncing colleagues, husbands denouncing wives and wives denouncing husbands, subordinates denouncing chiefs and chiefs denouncing subordinates'. Lurking in the background is the apocryphal tale of Pavlik Morozov, the thirteen-year-old Soviet schoolboy who, in 1932, was said to have denounced his father to the authorities and was in turn killed by his family. There is also an awareness of the fate of poets, writers and artists in the Soviet Union and Nazi Germany. At the time she wrote the book, Boye did not know of the ultimate fate of Jews in Germany and Nazi-occupied Europe, and so that dimension is missing from the narrative, though in the occasional references to the 'border peoples' there are hints at something of the kind. Boye's friend Ekelöf also saw a prophecy of the destruction of Hiroshima, half a decade before it took place, in the dream sequence that forms the centre of Chapter Fourteen, in which Kall walks through a ruined city, poisoned by noxious fumes.[6]

The possibility that there may be an escape from the moral and existential death trap of the World State is evinced by the themes of love and personal liberation that run through

Kallocain and are a constant motif in Karin Boye's poetry and fiction,[7] as exemplified in her 1934 novel *Kris* (*Crisis*). The book charts the religious, emotional and psychological development of a twenty-year-old woman in a Lutheran seminary, and is really a kind of semi-fictional, semi-autobiographical diary. It mirrors Boye's own progression, from an enclosed psyche in thrall to a divine will towards the liberation of personality, an opening to the world, and a resistance to an oppressive, patriarchal social and educational structure. The story focuses on a homosexual relationship, as Malin Forst, the novel's first-person narrator, develops an infatuation with Siv, a beautiful fellow student. Gradually, the infatuation becomes something more meaningful: through her involvement with Siv, Malin gains a liberation of self, and, through the psychological crisis, a sense of personal identity.

Beside and behind the main narrative of Leo Kall and the truth drug, *Kallocain* also tells the story of a woman, Leo's wife, Linda, who finds her way to freedom and authenticity in spite of social oppression and overwhelming historical odds. Linda makes a decision to follow her heart and join the dimly glimpsed but nonetheless real community of dissidents and resistance fighters. She also establishes inner contact with a vegetal, plant-like, growing and living reality that undermines and subverts the inhuman surface of the World State, and by doing so contradicts the mechanical, male-dominated totalitarian system – she is now on her way 'somewhere'.

Linda's search for freedom and authenticity reflects the dominant note in Boye's life and work. She lived in an era in which creating art that spoke out for truth and personal liberation could in itself be a heroic act. Peter Weiss, the German writer, artist and experimental film-maker (who adopted Swedish nationality), recognized this when he recreated Karin Boye as a character in the third volume (as yet untranslated into English) of his tripartite novel *Die Ästhetik des Widerstands* (*The Aesthetics of Resistance*, 1975–1981). In 1939, at the age of twenty-two, after periods of residence with his family in England and in Czechoslovakia, fleeing Nazi persecution, Weiss moved to the small township of Alingsås, near

Göteborg, Sweden, where his father ran a textile factory. Alingsås was at that time where the writer and theologian Anita Nathorst, Karin Boye's friend and counsellor, had her home, and Boye visited the town regularly to stay with her. It appears that during 1939 and 1940, Boye and Weiss met and formed a brief friendship that was broken when Boye ended her life in Alingsås in 1941. Weiss's clear and vivid portrait of her in his novel seems to be drawn from lived reality:

> This woman, still young, with a small, delicate figure, a thin, boyish countenance, short-cut dark hair, dark eyes, and heavily drawn black eyebrows, sat quietly beside my mother, looking at her and stroking her hands from time to time. I learned that it was the writer Boye, who lived in Bratt's guest house. Her shyness prevented the start of a conversation for a long time, yet she had an almost single-minded devotion to my mother, and not until the autumn, once when she had come alone and I accompanied her to the street, did we exchange a few words, and entered into a dialogue that was initially hesitant but became more and more extensive, lasting – each time interrupted for a month – until the end of March Nineteen Hundred and Forty-One . . . [8]

Weiss's anonymous narrator says that, at some deep psychological level, Boye wanted to fuse with the masses, but that, in the context of the world situation, was not motivated by a desire for life – rather, by a mounting despair and a wish for disappearance and annihilation. Nevertheless, in Weiss's novel, Boye is a heroic figure who stands alongside members of the real-life 'Rote Kapelle', or Red Orchestra – some 400 people who resisted the Nazi regime in various capacities. Many of these resisters had connections in Sweden, and moved between Sweden and Germany in secret. In Weiss's novel, Boye is included in their ranks as a brave fighter against fascism who, like them, has acquired an almost legendary status in world history:

> What she portrayed was not utopia, as I had assumed, but examination of the present day; the time-shifts that seemed to cause a detachment from our reality pointed to what existed now. The

guilt that she carried within her was less about sexual conflicts than about being party to the inability of people to stop the development of the state into an instrument of murder.[9]

Kallocain is the summation of Karin Boye's poetic and literary career, and also her testament as a human being. While before in her writing she had sought to build an inner cosmos, a realm accessed by hymn-like poems that moved beyond and behind physical reality, in *Kallocain* she portrayed the reality of the contemporary world in terms of a dreamlike, psychoanalytic vision that reproduced the features of collectivist society while also reflecting the ethical and spiritual conflicts on which her poetry was founded. This gave her the strength to defy the oncoming demons in the outside world with a conviction that external reality was only *apparently* invincible: the intense, inner idealism of her poetic credo asserts itself in the story of Linda and her journey towards the 'fools' – the dissidents capable of building an alternative society, even if their struggle is wrought at the expense of their own lives. By courageously submitting to their fate, the dissidents nonetheless survive and fulfil the conditions of T. S. Eliot's mantra-like phrase quoted in the epigraph: 'the awful daring of a moment's surrender'. Beyond the pall of hopelessness in which the novel at times appears shrouded, there is a glimmer of hope. Under the influence of the truth drug, Rissen says:

I'm a cog. I'm a creature from which they have taken the life . . . And yet: right now I know that it isn't true. It's the Kallocain that's making me full of irrational hope, of course – everything is becoming light and clear and calm. At least I'm alive – in spite of all they have taken from me – and right now I know that *what I am is on the way somewhere*. I have seen death's power spread out across the world in wider and wider circles – but must not life's power also have its circles, even though I haven't been able to see them? . . . Yes, yes, I know that it's the effect of the Kallocain, but can't it be true, even so?

NOTES

1. Margit Abenius: *Drabbad av renhet* ([Afflicted by Purity], Bonniers, 1950), my translation. No full-length biography of Karin Boye exists in English. The major biographical studies by Margit Abenius (*Drabbad av renhet*) and Johan Svedjedal (*Den nya dagen gryr* [The New Day Dawns] Wahlström & Widstrand, 2017) still await translation. A condensed English-language biography forms the introduction to *Karin Boye: Complete Poems* (Bloodaxe, 1994).

2. Quoted in Svedjedal, op. cit.

3. Abenius, op. cit.

4. Erika Gottlieb: *Dystopian Fiction East and West: Universe of Terror and Trial* (McGill-Queen's University Press, 2001).

5. Gunnar Ekelöf: 'Kallocain' in *Blandade kort* (Bonniers, 1957).

6. Ekelöf, op. cit.

7. Boye's concept of love was derived from Buddhism and Sufi mysticism, and it embraced a very wide spectrum of experience, thought and emotion. Ultimately it was a semi-religious concept that appealed to figures like UN Secretary-General Dag Hammarskjöld, who mentioned, discussed and quoted her poetry in his diaries. See Dag Hammarskjöld, tr. Leif Sjöberg and W. H. Auden, *Markings* (Faber & Faber, 1964).

8. Peter Weiss: *Die Ästhetik des Widerstands* [The Aesthetics of Resistance] (Suhrkamp, 1975–81), my translation.

9. Peter Weiss: op. cit., my translation.

Chronology

1900	26 October: Karin Boye born in Gothenburg, Sweden.
1903	Birth of brother, Sven.
1904	Birth of brother, Ulf.
1909	Family moves to Stockholm. Boye starts writing poetry from age of ten.
1915	Family moves to Huddinge, in the countryside near Stockholm.
1921	After graduating from college in Stockholm, moves to Uppsala, where she studies Greek, Scandinavian languages and literary history. Becomes a member of the international socialist and pacifist organization Clarté. Also active in a small group of students called the Poets' Corner, and gives talks and writes articles.
1922	Publication of *Clouds* (*Moln*; poetry).
1924	Publication of *Hidden Lands* (*Gömda land*; poetry).
1926	Gains her Bachelor of Arts degree at Uppsala. Moves back to Huddinge and studies history at Stockholm University.
1927	Gains Bachelor of Arts degree in history at Stockholm University. Publication of *The Hearths* (*Härdarna*; poetry).
1928–30	Member of the editorial staff of Clarté.
1928	Becomes engaged to the author Leif Björk and takes part in a three-week study tour of the Soviet Union.
1929	Works as a teacher at the secondary school in Motala. Marriage to Leif Björk.

1930   Visits Yugoslavia with her husband. Impressions
        from the journey form part of the essay collection
        Varia (1949).
        Leaves Clarté.
1931   Publication of *Astarte* (novel).
        Becomes a member of the literary society 'The Nine'
        and starts the literary magazine *Spektrum* with Erik
        Mesterton and Josef Riwkin, which will introduce
        T. S. Eliot and the surrealists to Swedish readers.
        With Mesterton, translates T. S. Eliot's *The Waste
        Land*.
1932   Separates from husband.
1932–3 Lives in Germany, where she undergoes psycho-
        analysis in Berlin. Meets Margot Hanel, with whom
        she lives for the rest of her life.
1933   October: Leaves Germany and returns to Stock-
        holm. Leaves *Spektrum*.
        Publication of *Merit Awakes* (*Merit vaknar*; novel).
1934   Divorce from husband finalized.
        Publication of *Crisis* (*Kris*; novel) and *Settlements*
        (*Uppgörelser*; short stories).
1935   Publication of *For the Tree's Sake* (*För trädets skull*;
        poetry).
1936   Publication of *Too Little* (*För lite*; novel).
1938   Travels to Greece over summer.
1940   Publication of *Kallocain* (novel) and *Out of Order*
        (*Ur funktion*; short stories). Brief friendship with
        Peter Weiss.
1941   23 April: Is found dead in open country near Aling-
        sås in circumstances that are still unclear. Hanel
        commits suicide shortly after.
        Posthumous publication of *The Seven Deadly Sins
        and Other Poems* (*De sju dödssynderna och
        andra dikter*, ed. Hjalmar Gullberg; poetry) and
        Annunciation (*Bebådelse*; a collection including
        the eponymous novella and some short stories).
1949   Essays and other minor texts published in *Tendency
        and Effect* (*Tendens och verkan*) and *Varia*.

KALLOCAIN

The awful daring of a moment's surrender
By this and this only we have existed.

(T. S. Eliot: *The Waste Land*)

CHAPTER I

The book I now sit down to write will inevitably appear pointless to many – if indeed I dare suppose that 'many' will ever have a chance to read it – since quite on my own initiative, without anyone's orders, I am beginning a task of this kind and yet am myself not really clear about its purpose. I will and must, and that is all. Ever more inexorable are the demands for purpose and method in what is done and said, so that not a word shall fall at random – it is only the author of this book who has been compelled to go the other way, out into futility. For although my years here as prisoner and chemist – they must be over twenty, I imagine – have been full enough of work and hurry, there must be something that feels this to be insufficient, and has directed and envisioned another task within me, one that I myself had no possibility of envisioning, and in which I nevertheless have had a deep and almost painful interest. That task will be completed when I have written my book. So although I realize how absurd my writings must appear in the light of all rational and practical thinking, I shall write all the same.

Perhaps I would not have dared to do it before. Perhaps imprisonment has simply made me light-headed. My living conditions now are not very different from those I experienced as a free man. The food turned out to be slightly worse here – I got used to that. The bunk turned out to be somewhat harder than my bed back home in Chemistry City No. 4 – I got used to that. I was able to go out in the open air somewhat more rarely – that, too, I got used to. The worst thing was the separation from my wife and children, particularly as I knew and still know nothing of their fate: this was something that filled the first years of my imprisonment with worry and anxiety. But in time I began to feel calmer than before, and increasingly comfortable with my existence. Here I had nothing to worry about. I had neither subordinates nor superiors – apart from the prison guards, who seldom disturbed my work, and concerned themselves merely with seeing that I obeyed the regulations. I had neither protectors nor rivals. The scientists with whom I was sometimes brought together, so that I could keep abreast of new research in the field of chemistry, treated me with polite dispassion, apart from some condescension because of my foreign nationality. I knew that none of them thought they had any reason to envy me. To put it briefly: in a way I sometimes felt that I was freer than I would be in freedom. But alongside the calm, there also grew within me this strange labour with the past, and now I shall be unable to rest until I have written down my memories from a certain eventful period in my life. Because of my scientific work it has been made possible for me to write, and there is no inspection until the moment I deliver a completed assignment. So I can afford myself this single pleasure, even though it may be the last one I am granted.

At the time my story begins I was approaching my forties. Perhaps if I am to introduce myself I may tell you about the image I had of life. There are few things that say more about a person than their image of life: whether they see it as a road, a battlefield, a growing tree or a rolling sea. For my part I saw it with the eyes of a well-behaved schoolboy, as a staircase up which you hurried from landing to landing as fast as you could, panting for breath and with your rival at your heels. In actual fact I had few rivals. Most of my colleagues at the laboratory had invested all their ambition in the military, and viewed their day's work as a tedious but necessary diversion from the evening's military duties. I would not have liked to admit to any of them how much more interested I was in my chemistry than in my military service, though I was by no means a bad soldier. At any rate, I kept on climbing my staircase at full tilt. How many stairs had to be climbed was something I had never considered, let alone what wonderful things might be in the attic. Perhaps I hazily imagined the house of life as similar to one of our

ordinary city buildings, where you climbed up out of the bowels of the earth and finally emerged on the roof terrace in the
open air, in wind and daylight. What the wind and the daylight
would correspond to in my life's journey I had no clear idea.
But it was certain that each new landing on the staircase was
marked by short official messages from higher up: about a successful exam, a passed test, a transfer to a more important field
of activity. I also had a whole series of such life-altering endings
and beginnings behind me, yet not so many that a new one
would lose its significance beside them. It was therefore with a
dash of fever in my blood that I returned from the short telephone call informing me that I might expect my control chief to
arrive the following day, and so could start experimenting on
human material. Thus, tomorrow the final and crucial test of
my greatest discovery to date would take place.

Such was my elation that during the ten minutes that still
remained of my working hours I found it hard to make a start
on anything new. Instead, I cheated a little – for the first time
in my life, I believe – and began to put the apparatus away
early, slowly and carefully, while stealing a glance through the
glass walls on both sides to see if anyone had noticed me. As
soon as the bell rang to announce that work was over for the
day, I hurried out through the long laboratory corridors, where
I was one of the first in the stream. I quickly showered, changed
out of my work clothes and into my leisure uniform, jumped
into the paternoster lift and a few moments later was up on the
street. As our apartment had been allocated in the district where
my work was, we had surface permits there, and I always enjoyed
the chance to stretch my legs in the fresh air.

As I was passing the metro station it occurred to me that I
might as well wait for Linda. Since I was so early, she had probably not yet got home from her food factory, over twenty minutes'
metro ride away. A train had recently arrived, and a flood of
people welled up out of the ground, squeezed through the bar-
riers, where the surface permits were checked, and trickled out
over the surrounding streets. Over the now empty roof terraces,
over all the rolled-up dark-grey and meadow-green tarpaulins,
which in the space of ten minutes could render the city invisible

from the air, I watched the swarming horde of homeward-bound fellow soldiers in leisure uniform, and it suddenly struck me that perhaps they all had the same dream that I had: the dream of the way up.

The thought gripped me. I knew that in the olden days, during the civilian era, people had to be lured to work and exertion by the hope of more spacious accommodation, better food and more attractive clothes. Nowadays nothing like that was needed. The standard apartment – one room for the unmarried, two for families – was sufficient for all, from the lowliest to the most deserving. The food from the house kitchen brought satiety to the general as well as to the private. The regular uniform – one for work, one for leisure and one for the military and police service – was the same for all, for man and woman, and for high and low, except for the rank markings. Even the latter were no more ostentatious for one person than for another. The desirable feature of a higher executive marking lay only in what it symbolized. So loftily ethereal is each single fellow soldier in the World State, I mused happily to myself, that what he considers to possess the highest value has no more tangible form for him than three black loops upon his sleeve – three black loops that are a pledge both of his own self-respect and of respect from others. It is indeed possible to have enough of material comforts, and more than enough – and for precisely that reason I suspect that the old civilian capitalist twelve-room apartments were scarcely more than a symbol – but of this most subtle distinction of all, which is pursued in the form of rank markings, no one can have too much. No one can have so much respect and so much self-respect that they do not want more. On the things that are most ethereal, most evanescent and elusive of all does our unshakable social order rest securely for all time.

Immersed in such reflections I stood by the metro exit, observing, as in a dream, the guards patrolling to and fro along the barbed-wire-crested district wall. By the time that Linda finally passed through the barrier four trains had arrived, four times the cohorts had streamed up into the daylight. I hurried over to her and we continued side by side.

We could not talk, of course, because of the air force exercises, which permitted no conversation to be held out of doors either by day or by night. At any rate, she saw my pleased expression and nodded encouragingly, though serious as always. Not until we had entered the building and the lift had taken us down to our apartment did a relative silence enclose us – the rumble of the metro, which shook the walls, was still sufficiently muffled for us to be able to converse unhindered – and yet we were careful to delay all talk until we were inside the apartment. Had anyone heard us talking in the lift, they would quite naturally have suspected that we were discussing matters we did not want the children or the home help to hear. There had been cases where enemies of the state and other criminals tried to use the lift as a conspirators' den; after all, it was an obvious choice, as for technical reasons police ears and police eyes could not be installed in a lift, and the concierge usually had other things to do than run up and down listening on the landings. So we took care to say nothing until we entered the family room, where that week's home help had already set the table for dinner and was waiting with the children, whom she had fetched down from the residents' creche. She seemed to be a nice, orderly girl, and our friendly greeting was prompted by more than our awareness that she, like all home helps, was duty-bound to deliver a report on the family at the end of the week – a reform generally considered to have improved the ambience in many homes. An aura of happiness and well-being reigned around our table, especially as our eldest son Ossu was present among us. He had arrived on a visit from the children's camp, as it was a home evening.

'I have something pleasant to tell you,' I said to Linda over the potato soup. 'My experiment has reached the point where I can start using human material tomorrow, under the supervision of a control chief.'

'Who do you think it will be?' asked Linda.

I am certain that I showed no reaction, but inwardly her words made me jump. It could have been a perfectly innocent question. What was more natural than a wife asking her husband who his control chief would be? After all, the length of the testing period depended on how petty-minded or how easygoing the control chief happened to be. There had even been cases where ambitious control chiefs had made the research-er's discovery their own, and there were relatively few ways to protect oneself from this. Not surprising, then, that one's near-est and dearest should ask who it was going to be.

But I listened out for an undertone in her voice. My most immediate chief, and therefore probably my future control chief, was Edo Rissen. And Edo Rissen had previously been employed at the food factory where Linda worked. I knew that they had had a fair amount of contact with each other, and from various small signs I concluded that he had made a cer-tain impression on my wife.

At her question my jealousy awoke and pricked up its ears. How intimate, really, was the relationship between her and Ris-sen? In a large factory it could often happen that two people were out of sight of the others, in the storage rooms, for example, where bales and crates blocked the view through the glass walls and where, moreover, no one else was busy at the time . . . . . Also, I knew for a fact that Linda had often done shifts as a night guard at the factory. Rissen could easily have had his shift at the same time. Anything was possible, even the worst of all: that it was still him she loved, and not me.

At that time I seldom wondered about myself, about what I thought and felt or what other people thought and felt, unless it had a direct practical significance for me. Only later, during my lonely time as a prisoner, did the moments begin to return as riddles, forcing me to wonder, interpret and reinterpret. Now, so long after the event, I know that when I so eagerly hoped for 'certainty' in the question of Linda and Rissen, I did not really want a certainty that there was no relationship between them. I wanted certainty that she had moved away from me. I wanted a certainty that would bring an end to my marriage.

But at that time I would have rejected such a thought with contempt. Linda played too important a role in my life, I would have said. And it was true, and no brooding and no reinterpre-tations have since been able to alter *that*. In terms of importance she might easily have competed with my career. Against my will she held on to me in a way that was quite irrational.

One can talk of 'love' as an outdated, romantic concept, but I am afraid it exists all the same, and right from the outset it contains an element that is indescribably painful. A man is attracted to a woman, a woman to a man, and with each step they take towards each other they lose something of themselves: a series of defeats, where they had hoped for victories. Already in my first marriage – a childless one, and therefore not something to be continued – I had experienced a foretaste. Linda increased it to a nightmare. During the first years of our marriage I really did have a nightmare, though I did not connect it with her: I stood in a great darkness, powerfully illuminated by spotlights; from out of the darkness I felt the Eyes directed at me, and I wriggled like a worm to get away, but I could not avoid feeling mortified with shame at the indecent rags I was wearing. Only later did I realize that it was a good picture of my relationship with Linda, in which I felt myself to be frighteningly transparent, though I did everything I could to creep away and protect myself, while she seemed to remain the same enigma; wonderful, strong, almost superhuman, but eternally disturbing because her enigmatic quality gave her a hateful superiority. When her mouth contracted into a narrow red line – no, it was not a smile, either of scorn or of joy, it could rather be called a tension, as when one tenses a bow – and meanwhile her eyes remained frozen, wide open – then the same ripple of dread passed through me again and again, and she continued to bind me and draw me to her with the same mercilessness, although I knew that she would never open herself to me. I suppose it is right to use the word 'love' when in the midst of hopelessness one clings to the other person, as if in spite of everything a miracle could happen – when the pain itself has acquired a sort of value of its own and become a testimony to the fact that one has at least one thing in common with the other person: the expectation of something that does not exist.

Around us we saw parents divorce as soon as their batch of children was ready for the children's camp – divorce and remarry, to produce more batches. Ossu, our eldest, was already eight, and so had been in the children's camp for a year. Laila, the youngest, was four, and still had three years left at home.

And then? Would we also divorce and remarry, in the childish belief that the same expectation might be less hopeless with someone else? All the reason I possessed told me that it was a deceptive illusion. A single, small irrational hope whispered: no, no, the reason you have failed with Linda is because she wants to go to Rissen! She belongs to Rissen, not to you! Be clear about the fact that it's Rissen she is thinking of – then it will all be explained, and you will still have hope for a love that has some meaning!

It was so strangely convoluted, this thing that awoke with Linda's self-evident question.

'I suppose it will be Rissen,' I replied, and listened eagerly to the silence that followed.

'Is it indiscreet to ask what sort of experiment it is?' the home help asked.

She had a perfect right to ask, of course, for in a way she was there precisely in order to keep track of what transpired in the family. And I could not see anything that could be twisted and used against me, nor any way in which it could harm the State if the rumour of my discovery were to spread in advance.

'It's something that I hope will benefit the State,' I said. 'A drug that will make any person reveal their secrets, all that they previously kept to themselves in silence, out of shame or fear. Are you from this city, Fellow Soldier Home Help?'

Now and again one came across people who had been brought here in times of manpower shortage and who therefore did not have the general education of the chemistry cities, except what they managed to pick up at an adult age.

'No,' she said, blushing. 'I'm from outside.'

Precise explanations of where one was from were strictly forbidden, as they could be used for purposes of espionage. That, of course, was why she had blushed.

'Then I shall not go into detail regarding the chemical compound or its manufacture,' I said. 'And perhaps one should avoid doing that anyway, for under no circumstances must the substance fall into private hands. But possibly you have heard how in the olden days alcohol was used as an intoxicant, and what effects it had?'

'Yes,' she said. 'I know that it made their homes unhappy, ruined their health, and in the worst cases led to tremors in the whole body and hallucinations about white mice, chickens and the like.'

I recognized the wording of the very elementary textbooks and smiled quietly. She had clearly not yet managed to acquire the general education of the chemistry cities.

'That's right,' I said. 'That's how it was in the worst cases. But before it went that far, it often happened that the intoxicated people talked indiscreetly, betrayed secrets and did incautious things, as their capacity for shame and fear was removed. Those are the effects my drug has – at least I believe so, for I haven't yet been able to conduct conclusive tests. But the difference is that it isn't swallowed, but is injected directly into the blood and actually has quite a different chemical composition. It also lacks the unpleasant after-effects you mentioned – at least, one doesn't have to administer such large doses. A slight headache is all that the test subject feels afterwards, and there is no incidence, as there sometimes was with alcohol-intoxicated subjects, of people being unable to remember what they said. I think you will understand that it's an important discovery. From now on no criminal will be able to deny the truth. Not even our most intimate thoughts will be our own any more – as we have for so long believed, mistakenly.'

'Mistakenly?'

'Yes, indeed, mistakenly. Words and actions are born of thoughts and feelings. Then how should thoughts and feelings be the private concern of the individual? Does not the whole of the fellow soldier belong to the State? To whom would his thoughts and feelings belong, if not to the State? It's merely that until now it has not been possible to control them – but now the drug has been discovered.'

She gave me a hurried look, but lowered it at once. Not a line in her demeanour changed, but I had the impression that her colour faded.

'You have nothing to be afraid of, Fellow Soldier,' I said to her, encouragingly. 'There are no plans to lay bare all the individual's little likes and dislikes. If my discovery were to end up in private hands – yes, then one might easily imagine the chaos that would ensue! But of course that must not happen. The drug must serve our security, everyone's security, the State's security.'

'I am not afraid, I have nothing to be afraid of,' she replied rather coldly, and yet I had only meant to be friendly.

So then we moved on to other subjects of conversation. The children told us what had they had done during their day at the creche. They had played in the play-tank, an enormous enamel basin some four square metres wide and one metre deep, in which one could not only drop small toy bombs, setting fire to forests and rooftops made of flammable material, but could also enact entire naval battles in miniature if one filled the tank with water and loaded the cannons of the little vessels with the same weak explosive that was used in the toy bombs; there were even torpedo boats. In this way strategic vision was inculcated in the children by means of play, so that it became second nature to them, almost an instinct, and at the same time it was, after all, fun of the first order. Sometimes I envied my own children for growing up with such a sophisticated toy – in my own childhood the mild explosive had not yet been invented – and I found it rather hard to comprehend the fact that they longed with all their hearts to reach the age of seven and join the children's camp, where the exercises were more reminiscent of military training, and where they would stay both day and night.

It often seemed to me that the new generation took a more realistic view of life than we had in our childhood. On the particular day I am talking about I acquired new evidence that this was so. As it was a family evening, when neither Linda nor I had police or military duty, and Ossu, my eldest, was visiting us at home – thus was the family's intimate life catered for – I thought of a way of entertaining the children. From the laboratory I had procured a very small amount of sodium, which I planned to put in the water and sail around with its pale violet flame. We prepared a full tank, put out the lights, and gathered around my little chemical marvel. I myself had been very fond of the phenomenon as a child when my father showed it to me, but for my own children it was quite definitely a flop. Ossu, who was already allowed to make fires on his own, shoot a toy pistol and throw small firecrackers that were meant to be hand grenades – well, it was perhaps quite natural that he did not appreciate the small pale flame. But that four-year-old Laila was not interested in an explosion unless it cost the lives of several enemies – that astonished me. The only one of the children who seemed to be fascinated was Maryl, our middle daughter. She sat still and dreamy as usual, watching the sizzling jack-o'-lantern with wide-open eyes that reminded me of her mother's. And although I suppose her attentiveness brought me a certain consolation, at the same time it worried me. With unambiguous clarity it dawned on me that it was Ossu and Laila who were the children of the new era. Their attitude was the correct and objective one, while mine was a manifestation of obsolete romanticism. And in spite of the sense of justification she gave me, I suddenly wished that Maryl were more like the others. It did not bode well that she should fall outside the healthy development of the generations in this way.

The evening went by, and then it was time for Ossu to go back to the children's camp. If he wanted to stay, or was afraid of the long metro journey, he did not show it. With his eight years he was already a disciplined fellow soldier. Through me, on the other hand, passed a hot wave of longing for the days when all three snuggled down in their little beds. A son is a son, after all, I thought, and he is closer to his father than the daughters are. And yet I did not dare to think of the day when Maryl too, and Laila, would be gone and only come home two evenings a week to say hello. At any rate, I took care not to let anyone notice my weakness. The children should not one day complain about my bad example, the home help should not be able to report a slack attitude on the part of the family head, and Linda – Linda least of all! I did not want to be despised by anyone, but least of all by Linda, she who was never weak.

So the beds in the family room were folded out from the wall and made up for the little girls, and Linda tucked them both in. The home help had just put the dishes and the remains of our dinner in the dumb waiter and was getting ready to leave when something occurred to her.

'That's right,' she said, 'there's a letter for you, my chief. I put it in the parents' room.'

Somewhat surprised, Linda and I inspected the letter, an official one. Had I been the home help's police supervisor I would probably have given her a warning for this. Whether she had really forgotten all about it or deliberately neglected it, it was still careless of her not to check what an official letter contained – she was completely within her rights to do so. But at the same time I had a fleeting sense that the contents of the letter might be such that I ought to be grateful to her for having shirked her duty.

The letter was from the Seventh Bureau of the Ministry of Propaganda. And in order to explain its contents I must go back a little in time.

CHAPTER 2

It had happened at a celebration two months earlier. One of the youth camp's assembly halls was decorated with long banners in the colours that are those of the State. Sketches were performed, speeches delivered, people marched through the hall to the beat of the drum and dined together. The occasion for all this was that a group of girls in the youth camp had received orders that they were to be transferred, no one really knew where. Some rumours said that it might be another chemistry city, others that it was one of the shoe cities, or at any rate a place where there was a deficit both in terms of labour force and of male versus female ratios. And so from our city, and presumably a number of others, too, young women were assembled and sent there so that the numbers that once had been established might be maintained. And what was now taking place was the farewell banquet for those who had been called up.

Festivities of this kind always bore a certain resemblance to the banquets that are held for departing soldiers. True, there was one major difference: at events like this, everyone – both those who were going away and those who were staying behind – knew that not a hair of the heads of the young people who were leaving their home city would be harmed. On the contrary, everything would be done to ensure that they quickly and easily became a part of their new surroundings and that before long they felt perfectly at home there. The similarity lay only in the fact that both parties knew with almost one hundred per cent certainty that they would never see one another again. For no connection between the cities was permitted other than the official one, entrusted to the hands of sworn and strictly supervised officials, in the interests of preventing espionage. And even if one or another of the conscripted young people really did end up in the transport service – an extremely unlikely event, as the transport officials were nearly always nursed into their vocation from infancy in special transport education cities – then it would have required a peculiar coincidence for them to be employed on one of the transport lines that led to their home city, and for their free time to be spent in their home city. This applied only to the land transport staff – for the airline staff lived in complete separation from their families, and under constant surveillance. In other words, it would have required miracles of chance for the parents to see their children again once those children had been moved to a different location. Viewed apart from this – yes, truly viewed apart from it, for one had no right to linger on the gloomier views on such a day – the banquet was a rollicking feast of joy, as was fitting when something happened that brought benefit and prosperity to the State.

Had I myself been among the happy celebrants, events would probably never have developed as they did. The hope of a good meal – at such occasions the food is always abundant and well-prepared, and the participants usually throw themselves on it like ravenous wolves – the drum, the speeches, the festive crowd itself, the unanimous cries – it all sent the hall into a great common ecstasy, as was traditional and desirable. However, I was not among the parents, the brothers and sisters, or the youth leaders. The evening was one of the four each week when I did military and police duty, and I was there quite simply in my capacity of police secretary. This meant that not only did I have a seat of my own on one of the four small corner platforms, where my task was to compile a report on the event, together with three other police secretaries in the other three corners, but also that it was my duty to keep a clear head in order to be able to conduct various observations on what happened in the hall. If any noisy dispute broke out, if anything suspicious took place – if, for example, one of the participants tried to leave after the end of the roll-call, it was a great help to the chairman and the doormen, who might often be engaged on some practical detail, to have four police secretaries watching over the

hall from a more or less secluded spot. So there I sat in my isolation, letting my gaze travel across the multitude, and although
on the one hand I should have liked to join in myself and share
in the communal jubilation, I think that my sacrifice was offset
rather well by the awareness of my importance and dignity. In
fact, later in the evening one is normally relieved by another
official, so that one may after all partake of the meal, and is
then at least free to cast off all apprehension.

The young girls saying farewell were scarcely more than some
fifty in number, and you could easily distinguish them in the
crowd by their gilded festive crowns, which the city usually lent
out especially for events like this. One of the girls in particular
awoke my idle attention, perhaps because she was unusually
attractive, perhaps also because there was a lively restlessness,
like a secret fire, in her gaze and movements. Several times I
caught her darting searching glances in the direction of the
boys – this was at the beginning of the event, while the sketches
were being performed and the boys and girls from their different
camps still sat in separate groups – until at last she seemed to
find what she was seeking, and the fire in her movements grew
still, appearing to break out in a single clear, calm flame. I also
thought I could discern the face she had sought and found: so
painfully serious amid all the expectant and happy ones that
one almost felt sorry for the two of them. As soon as the last
sketch came to an end and the young people mingled with one
another, I saw them both cleave the multitude as though it were
water, and with almost blind certainty meet more or less in the
middle of the hall, in solitary stillness among all the shouting
and singing people. They stood in the midst of the commotion
as on a quiet rocky reef, not knowing in what space or what
time they existed.

I woke up and gave a snort at myself. They had succeeded in
dragging me away into their asocial world, torn free of the one
great sacrament for all: the community. I must have been very
tired, as just to sit and look at them had felt like resting. Sympathy was what they deserved least of all, those two, I thought.
Really, what can be more beneficial for a fellow soldier's character training than to grow accustomed at an early age to great

sacrifices for great goals? Think of all the people who spend the whole of their lives longing for a sacrifice that would be great enough! Envy was all I could give them, and there was probably also envy in the dissatisfaction I thought I detected among the comrades of the two young people – envy, and also a dash of contempt that so much time and energy were being wasted on one individual. I, for my part, was unable to view them with contempt. They were acting out an eternal drama, beautiful in its tragic inexorability.

At any rate I must have been tired, as my interest kept circling around the few elements of seriousness offered by the merry celebration. Only a few minutes after I had taken my eyes off the two young people, who as it happened had become separated by impatient comrades, my attention fastened instead on a thin, middle-aged woman, probably the mother of one of the conscripted girls. She too seemed in some way disconnected from the bustling collectivity. I don't really know how I realized this, for I should never have been able to prove it, as she continued to take part in the event, moving in time to the marchers, nodding along with the speakers, shouting with the shouters. But I somehow had a sense that she did this mechanically, that instead of being raised up by the liberating wave of the collective, in some way she stood outside it, even outside her own voice and her own movements, just as isolated as the two young people were. Those around her must have had the same feeling, for they attempted to approach her from different directions. Several times from my platform I saw someone take her by the arm and pull her along with them or stop and talk with her, but soon, disappointed, withdraw, even though her answers and smiles functioned impeccably. There was only one lively, ugly little man who would not let himself be frightened away so easily. When she fired off her weary smile at him and then resumed her even wearier solemnity, he remained standing unseen some distance away, watching her in obvious reflection.

In some way I felt close to the tired and isolated woman, though I could not work out why. In rational terms I could see that if the two young people were deserving of envy, she deserved it to an even higher degree: her self-sacrificing valour was greater than

theirs and with it also her strength and eminence. The young
people's emotion would, in spite of everything, soon fade away
and be replaced by some new ardour, and if they tried to preserve the memory, it would soon cease to be painful and become
merely beautiful and radiant, a resource in the monotony of the
everyday. Their mother's sacrifice might be so great that it
renewed itself each day. After all, I myself knew such a loss,
heavy enough, though one day I would probably succeed in
overcoming it – I mean the loss of Ossu, my eldest, and yet he
came home twice a week, and I really hoped I would be able to
keep him in Chemistry City No. 4, even when he was grown up.
Of course I knew that this attitude to the small fellow soldiers
one gave to the State was of too personal a nature, and I would
never have liked to show it openly, but in secret it cast a certain
aura over my life, perhaps not least because it was so entirely
secret and controlled. No doubt it was the same torment and
resource that I recognized in the woman, and also the same
silent self-control. I could not help putting myself in her place:
she would never be able to see her daughter again, not even hear
from her, as the post office censored private letters with ever
increasing severity, so that nowadays only really important
news, written in a brief and objective style and accompanied by
the proper verifications, were let through to the addressee. And
a somewhat presumptuous and individualistic-romantic thought
came to me, about a kind of 'compensation' that should accrue
to fellow soldiers for having sacrificed their sentimental life to
the State, and ought to consist of the loftiest and richest thing
one could strive for: honour. As honour was consolation enough
and more than enough for wounded warriors, why should it not
also be so for every fellow soldier who felt wounded inwardly?
It was a muddled and romantic thought, and later that evening
it led to an incautious act.

Then the hour of my replacement struck, and I gave up my
seat to another police secretary, stepped down into the multitude and tried to blend with the general enthusiasm. Perhaps I
was too tired and hungry for it to work. As luck would have it,
just then the dinner tables, set and laid, were wheeled in from
the kitchens along well-greased rails, and everyone gathered

their folding chairs around the splendours and delicacies. Whether it was by pure chance, or whether she deliberately sought me out, I do not know, but amusingly enough the woman I had noticed came and sat down directly opposite me. It was not impossible that she had seen me and had read sympathy in my face. On the other hand, it was probably not by pure chance that the lively, ugly little man, who had earlier observed her, also came over and plumped himself down right next to her.

To judge by his behaviour, he had determined to force out into the open the very thing the woman wished to conceal. Everything he said was innocent enough in itself, but had the effect of chafing the wound he sensed in his table companion. He talked sadly of the loneliness that awaited those young girls. In order to avoid the harmful formation of cliques, he said, the young people who had been transferred were kept out of one another's reach. Then there were the difficulties with the new climate and the new way of life. With regard to the shoe cities, about which there were many guesses – by the way, how could such a rumour get out, the journey's destination was, and ought to be, secret, and the guesses might just as well be false as true! – with regard to the shoe cities, while it was true that a few of them were located just as far south as Chemistry City No. 4, most of them lay far to the north and had a real Nordic climate, with long, hard, dark winters that might make any stranger depressed. Actually, the worst problem was probably the language. Alas, the official language of the vast World State had not managed to become a universal vehicle of conversation. In many places national languages were still spoken, and they differed enormously from one another. He personally had heard someone relate in confidence that one of the shoe cities had a very difficult language with stems and inflections quite different from those we were used to here. But of course you should never believe rumour mongers; the person in question might never even have been outside Chemistry City No. 4!

For a moment it fleetingly occurred to me that the little man's behaviour must have been caused by some kind of desire for revenge, but I soon had to give up that thought. From the woman's courteous and disparaging replies I realized that they had met recently, perhaps only this evening. And gradually I sensed how it all hung together: the man had absolutely no personal reason for what he did; all of his mercilessness was prompted by the purest concern for the State's best interests. He had no other end in view than to expose the woman, who nursed private-sentimental and asocial feelings, and put her to shame in an outburst of tears or a heated reply, so that later he could point to her and say: See what we still have and must tolerate among us! From that point of view the man's ambition became not only understandable but downright praiseworthy, and the parrying between him and the object of his attacks acquired a new, fundamental significance. I followed it attentively, and when in the end my sympathies remained on her side, it was no longer because of feeble compassion, but because of something I did not need to be ashamed of in front of anyone: admiration for the almost masculine superiority she demonstrated in warding off his blows. Not a twitch on her face disturbed the courteous smile, not a tremor in her voice penetrated the light, cool tone when she met his skilful thrusts with one reason for consolation more superficial than the last. After all, learning comes easily to the young, a northern climate is many times healthier than a southern one, in the World State no fellow soldier need feel lonely, and why do you lament that she may forget her family? In a transfer, nothing is more desirable.

I was quite disappointed when the elegant parrying was interrupted by a rough, red-haired man nearby:

'What sentimental coddling is this? Look here, Fellow Soldier, whatever your name is, why are you sitting here blackening the deeds of the State, and on such a day? And to one of the mothers, too! Now, if ever, is the time for rejoicing, not troubles and sighs!'

Just then the speeches were about to resume, and in my brain there arose the unfortunate decision to direct yet another blow at the little man. My duties for the evening were not really over yet, I was one of the official speakers, and so it came to pass that my speech, rather carefully prepared as it was, with gestures and all, acquired a fatefully improvised conclusion:

'And, Fellow Soldiers, their heroic deed grows no less because it is sometimes accompanied by pain. The warrior feels pain from his wounds, the fallen warrior's widow feels pain beneath her veil, even though her joy in serving the State compensates for this pain many times. Pain may then also be vouchsafed to those who must be parted in their working lives, in most cases forever. And if it is worthy of our acclaim, when mother and daughter, comrade and comrade, part with joy in their eyes and cheers on their lips, then it is no less worthy of our admiration if behind the joy and the cheers lies a sorrow, a controlled, a disavowed sorrow – and perhaps this sorrow is *more* worthy of our admiration because it is a greater sacrifice to the State.'

Exultant and approving as the crowd already was, it immediately burst into a storm of cheers and handclapping. But I saw that here and there among the hand-clappers there also sat some who defiantly kept their hands still. Perhaps a thousand clap, and two keep still – and then those two are more important than the thousand; obviously, as those two may mean two informers, while not one of the thousand will lift a finger to defend the one surrounded by applause, once he has been denounced – and in any case, how would they be able to? It will not be hard to understand, then, that it was not pleasant to stand there in the throes of emotion, all the time feeling the ugly little man's eyes like arrow-shots. I cast a swift glance at him almost in passing. Of course he was not clapping.

What I now faced was the evening's aftermath. Just who had informed on me it was not easy to say: it might not necessarily have been the little man. Yet it was quite plain that I had been denounced. In the document it said:

'Fellow Soldier Leo Kall, Chemistry City No. 4 – After investigating the content of your address at the Youth Camp's farewell banquet for conscripted employees on 19 April this year, the Seventh Bureau of the Ministry of Propaganda has decided to advise you of the following:

Just as a wholehearted warrior is always more effective than an ambivalent one, so must also a happy fellow soldier, who neither to himself nor to others admits that he is sacrificing anything, be of greater value than a despondent one who is weighed down by his so-called sacrifice, even though he conceals his despondency; and consequently we have no reason to elevate fellow soldiers who seek to conceal ambivalence, depression and personal sentimentality under a controlled mask of happiness, but only those who, happy through and through, have nothing to hide, whereas the exposure of the former is a praiseworthy action in the best interests of the State.

We expect you to take the earliest opportunity of apologizing to the same gathering that formed your audience, in so far as it is possible to have it reassembled, or, failing that, on local radio.

Seventh Bureau of the Ministry of Propaganda.'

CHAPTER 3

So violent was my reaction that I later felt ashamed in Linda's presence. That this should arrive today of all days, in the midst of my triumph! That in the midst of my greatest hopes I should be struck by such a blow! Beside myself as I was, I said various things that were probably ill-considered, and that today, in spite of my good memory, I have difficulty in remembering: that I was a lost man, my career destroyed, my future without honour, my great discovery feather-light compared to what would appear on my secret card in every police department in the World State, and so on. And when Linda tried to console me, I really did think at first that it was pure deceit, and that she was merely brooding about how best to leave the sinking ship, even though the children were still of home age.

'Soon everyone will know what subversive speeches I give,' I said bitterly. 'If you want a divorce, go ahead, don't worry about the children being young. After all, it's better for them to be fatherless than to live with a subversive individual like myself . . . . .'

'How you exaggerate,' said Linda, calmly. (I even still remember the very word. What convinced me of her sincerity was not the calmness, not the motherliness in the tone of her voice, it was the heavy, almost indifferent tiredness.) 'How you exaggerate. How many illustrious fellow soldiers do you suppose have had black marks put next to their names and have later exonerated themselves? Don't you remember all the people we heard reading out their apologies on the radio between 8 and 9 p.m. on Friday evenings? Surely you must realize that flawlessness is not what makes a good fellow soldier, least of all flawlessness in questions like this, where State ethical policy is still being formed?'

At last I calmed down and began to realize that she was right. In my shaken condition I promised us both that I would avail myself of the radio's apology programme as soon as possible. I even began, right there and then, to make a draft of my forthcoming speech.

'Now you're exaggerating again,' said Linda, who was leaning over my shoulder and reading what I wrote. 'One shouldn't be knocked too flat, either, and one shouldn't be a rubber band that can be stretched any way at all – then one will be suspected of being able to bounce back, too, in an unguarded moment. Believe me, Leo, things like this should not be written when one is as upset as you are now.'

She was right, and I was thankful she was there. She was wise – wise and strong. But why did she sound so tired?

'You're not ill, are you, Linda?' I asked, anxiously.

'Why would I be ill? We had a medical examination last week. I was prescribed some open-air radiation, but otherwise I had a clean bill of health.'

I got up and embraced her.

'Don't die on me,' I said. 'I need you. You must stay with me.'

But alongside my fear of being left alone ran a tiny rivulet of hope: yes, why not – why could she not die – perhaps that would be the right solution to the problem? But I did not want to admit it. And so I pressed her to me, hard, in a kind of impotent rage.

We went to bed and put out the light. My monthly ration of sleeping pills had been used up long ago.

Even if her soft warmth and her fragrance, which was reminiscent of tea leaves, had not reached me in wave after wave under our shared duvet, I would have longed for her that night, for a closer closeness than gentle touching can give. The years had altered me. In my youth my senses were a kind of appendage, a demanding hanger-on who must be satisfied so I could get rid of him and be able to focus on other things, also a proud implement for pleasure, but not really a part of what I seriously called 'myself'. Now it was no longer like that. Fragrance and softness and pleasure were no longer the only things I wanted. The object of my flaring senses was something much harder to attain; it was the Linda who, for certain brief moments, I could glimpse behind the motionless wide-open eyes, behind the tensed red bow of a mouth, she who had let herself be glimpsed tonight, in her tone of tiredness, in her wise, calm counsel. And while the pulse-beats surged in my veins, I turned over on my other side and suppressed a sigh. I told myself that what I wanted from cohabitation between a man and a woman was merely a superstition, and nothing else, just as much of a superstition as when the savages of ancient times ate the hearts of their brave enemies in order to partake of their courage. There was no magical act that could give me the key and the title deeds to the paradise Linda was keeping from me. So then what was the point of it all?

On the wall sat the police ear and beside it the police eye, equally effective in darkness and in light. No one could think them anything but well-motivated: what hotbeds of espionage and conspiracy the parents' rooms might otherwise become, especially if they were also used as guest rooms! Later, when I obtained such an intimate view of the family lives of various fellow soldiers, I could not help making a close connection between the police ear and police eye and the unsatisfactory curve of the birth rate within the World State. But I hardly think it was because of them that my blood ran so thin nowadays. At least, it had never been like this before. Our World State certainly did not take an ascetic view of sex, for on the contrary the breeding of new fellow soldiers was a necessary and honourable task, and every effort was made to see to it that as soon as they reached the age of maturity men and women had an opportunity of fulfilling their duty in this regard. Also, from the very outset I had not objected to someone higher up making sure that I was a man. It had rather been a spur to action. Our nights had been bathed in a shimmer of ceremonial display, where the two of us were nothing but solemnly inspired and conscientious performers of a ritual in the sight of the State. But over the years a change had taken place. Whereas earlier, even in my most intimate activities, I had mainly speculated about how I was valued by the power that also made use of the eye on the wall, nowadays that power was increasingly becoming an oppressive encumbrance at precisely those moments when I yearned most wildly for Linda, and for the never-attained and never attainable miracle that would make me lord of her innermost mysteries. The eye I had wondered about was still there, but the eye was Linda herself. I began to sense that my love had taken an inappropriately private turn, and it weighed on my conscience. After all, the purpose of marriage was children – what did it have to do with superstitious dreams about keys and lordly dominions? Perhaps this dangerous turn in my marriage was one more reason for divorce. And inwardly I wondered if other divorces around us might have the same causes . . . . .

So I decided to sleep, but could not. Instead, the message from the Seventh Bureau of the Ministry of Propaganda began to dance around in my brain, until I no longer knew what side I wanted to lie on.

A wholehearted warrior is more effective than an ambivalent one: that is true, of course, that is logical. And what is to be done with the ambivalent ones? How are they to be made wholehearted?

A chilling discovery: there I lay, feeling worried about the ambivalent warriors, as if I were one of them. I must not drift in that direction. I did not want to be ambivalent, as a fellow soldier I was absolutely wholehearted, without a drop of deceit or treachery. Those who were useless must go, even she, the slim, self-controlled mother at the celebration. From now on my slogan would be: 'Shoot the ambivalent ones!' And your marriage? asked a malign little thought. But I gave it the reply it deserved: If my marriage did not improve, I would get a divorce. But not until the children were past home age.

And suddenly a realization flooded me with clarity and relief: my own discovery was wholly in line with the letter from the Seventh Bureau. Had not I myself talked to the home help today in the same vein? I would be believed and forgiven because of my discovery, I had shown myself to be reliable in action, and that possessed more weight than some random words at a stupid little dinner. In spite of everything I was a good fellow soldier, and perhaps capable of becoming an even better one.

Before I fell asleep I could not help chuckling to myself at a comical and gratifying fantasy, one of those whimsical images that pop up in the mind just before you drift off: I saw the ugly, lively little man from the celebratory dinner standing with a warning in his hand, and in a cold sweat: the big red-haired man had denounced him for his attempt to spoil the festivities, and blacken the actions of the State. That was worse, really . . .

CHAPTER 4

Not that I was in the habit of wasting time, either after morning exercises or otherwise, but that morning I think I took my shower with particular haste, and was putting on my work uniform in order to stand to attention when the door to my laboratory opened and the control chief walked in.

When he finally arrived it was Rissen, of course. Just as I had thought.

If I was disappointed, I hoped that at least it was not visible. There had been a small, faint possibility that it might be someone else, but it was Rissen, after all. And as he stood there before me, insignificant, almost hesitant in his bearing, I had a clear sense that I did not loathe him because there was possibly something going on between him and Linda, but that on the contrary I so disliked the notion of a relationship between them for the sole reason that it involved *him*. Anyone else, but not him. It was unlikely that Rissen would put any additional stumbling blocks in the way of my scientific career, he was too meek and biddable for that. But I would personally have preferred a less biddable and more devious control chief, one against whom I could have measured my own strength – if at the same time I could have had some respect for him. One could not respect Rissen, he was too unlike anyone else, he was too ridiculous. It was not so easy to express what was lacking in the man, but if you used the words 'in march-time', it gave you some idea. The determined comportment, the clear and measured manner of speaking that were the only natural and worthy attributes of a full-grown fellow soldier, were not at Rissen's disposal. Unexpectedly he could become far too eager, let his words stumble over one another, even render himself guilty of unintentional and comical gestures. From time to time he would make long, unmotivated pauses, subside into reflection and blurt out careless words that only the initiated could understand. When he heard people talking about something that was of particular interest to him, uncontrolled grimaces almost like those of an animal would cross his face, even in the presence of myself, a subordinate. On the one hand, I knew that as a scientist he had shining virtues; on the other, even though he was my chief I could not ignore the fact that there was a discrepancy between his value as a scientist and his value as a fellow soldier.

'Well, well,' he began in leisurely fashion, as if the working hours were his private property. 'Well, well. The fact is that I have been given a very detailed report on the whole of this matter. I think I have a clear idea of it now.'

And he began to repeat the more important points of my report.

'My chief,' I broke in impatiently. 'I have already taken the liberty of ordering five subjects from the Voluntary Sacrifice Service. They are sitting outside in the corridor, waiting.'

He gave me an ill-tempered look with his pensive eyes. I had the impression that he barely saw me. He was truly peculiar.

'Well, call one of them in, then,' he said. It sounded as though he were thinking out loud, not giving an order.

I pressed the button that rang the bell in the corridor. A moment later a man with his arm in a sling came in, halted inside the doorway, saluted and announced himself as 'No. 135 of the Voluntary Sacrifice Service'.

Slightly irritated, I asked if it had really been impossible to send a fresh test subject. In the course of my work as an assistant at one of the medical laboratories it had happened that my chief at the time had got hold of a woman whose entire glandular system had been wiped out by an earlier test, and I had a very clear recollection of how this kept distorting the result of his investigations. I did not want to risk something of that sort. As a matter of fact, I knew from the rules and regulations that one ought to firmly insist on one's right to have fresh test subjects: the habit of continually sending the same ones fostered a kind of cronyism, so that sometimes for long periods of time extremely conscientious and willing volunteers were denied the chance of showing their courage and obtaining some small extra earnings. A calling like the Voluntary Sacrifice Service was certainly more honourable than most, and ought to be seen as its own reward, if one were to be really strict about it – but then the salary was at the lower end of the scale, because of the many payments for injury compensation that were part and parcel of the profession.

The man stood to attention and apologized on behalf of his department. They really had no one else to send. There was a feverish amount of work going on in the poison gas laboratory just now, and the Voluntary Sacrifice Service was right in the front line, day in, day out, to the last man. As for No. 135 himself, he felt absolutely fine, except for a poison gas injury to his left hand, and as a personal apology he wished to say that as it ought to have healed long ago – even the chemist who had caused the injury was unable to say why it had not – he considered himself to be in the 'fresh' category, and hoped that the minor gas injury would not be a problem.

Indeed, it would not be a problem at all, so I calmed down.

'It's not your hands we need, but your nervous system,' I said. 'And in advance I can tell you that the experiment will not be painful, nor will it leave any damage, even of a temporary kind.'

No. 135 stood even more stiffly to attention, if that were possible. When he replied, his voice was almost like a fanfare:

'I regret that the State does not yet require a greater sacrifice from me: I am ready for anything.'

'Of course, I do not doubt it,' I said, in a serious tone.

I was convinced that he meant what he said. My only reservation was that he placed rather too much emphasis on his heroic courage. A scientist in his laboratory can be courageous, too, even though he has not been able to show it, I thought. As a matter of fact, it was not yet too late: what he had said about the feverish work at the poison gas laboratory was another sign that a war was coming. Another sign, one that I had noted to myself in private but had not wanted to discuss in order to avoid being seen as a pessimist and grumbler, was that during recent months the food had generally become much worse.

So I sat the man down in a comfortable chair that had been brought in especially for my experiments, rolled up his sleeve, washed the crook of his elbow, and injected the small syringe filled with its pale-green liquid. The second that No. 135 felt the prick of the needle his features grew taut, making them almost handsome. I must admit that I fancied I saw a hero on the chair before me. At the same time the colour drained from his face slightly, something unlikely to be caused by the pale-green liquid which could not yet have had time to take effect.

'How does that feel?' I asked, encouragingly, while the contents of the syringe dwindled. Again from the rules and regulations I knew that the test subject should be asked as many questions as possible, as it gave him a sense of equality and raised him above the pain in a certain way.

'Like normal, thank you!' No. 135 replied, but his speech was noticeably slower, as if to conceal the fact that his lips were trembling.

While he remained seated, waiting for the effects of the drug to take hold, we studied his card, which he had put down on the table. Year of birth, sex, racial type, body type, temperament type, blood type, and so on, peculiarities in the family, illnesses (a whole series of them, nearly all caused by experiments). I copied the essential information into my new and carefully arranged card system. The only thing that caused me some uncertainty was the year of birth, but it was probably correct, and I recalled that even back in my days as an assistant I had heard and observed that the test subjects in the Voluntary Sacrifice Service generally looked ten years older than they really were. When this was done I turned again to No. 135, who was beginning to twist and turn in his chair.

'Well?'

The man laughed in childish astonishment.

'I feel wonderful. I've never felt so good. But how afraid I am . . .'

The moment had arrived. We listened and paid attention. My heart was thumping. What if the man said nothing at all?

What if there was nothing he carried around in silence? What if what he was in the process of saying was nothing noteworthy at all? How then would my control chief ever be convinced? And how would I myself be sure? A theory, no matter how well-founded, is and remains a theory as long as it has not been proven. I could have been mistaken.

Then something happened for which I was not prepared. The big, coarse man began to sob inconsolably. He slid down in his chair, hanging over the armrest like a rag, and jerking slowly to and fro in rhythmical fashion, with long moans. I cannot express how painfully embarrassing it was, I did not know what to do with my body or my face. Rissen's self-control, I must admit, left nothing to be desired. If he was as uncomfortably affected as me, he hid it rather better.

This went on for several minutes. I felt ashamed before my chief, as though I could be held responsible for him having to witness such scenes. And yet I could not possibly know in advance what the test subjects would reveal, and neither I nor all the rest of our laboratory had any particular position of authority over them: they were sent out from a central agency in the middle of the laboratory district, so that they could be on hand for all the surrounding institutes.

At last he calmed down. The sobbing ebbed away, and he straightened up into a more dignified posture. Eager to bring an end to the embarrassing situation, I directed at him the first question I could think of:

'What's the matter?'

He directed his gaze towards us. One could see very well that he was conscious of our presence and our questions, even though he was not fully aware of who we were. When he answered, he turned distinctly to us, though not as one turns to one's superiors but as one addresses dreamed and nameless listeners.

'I am so unhappy,' he said impassively. 'I don't know what to do. I don't know how I am going to cope.'

'Cope with what?' I asked.

'This, all of it. I'm so afraid. I'm always so afraid. Not right now in particular, but in general, almost always.'

'Of the experiments?'

'Yes, of course, the experiments. Right now I don't know what I'm afraid of. Either it hurts or it doesn't so much, either you become a cripple or you get better again, either you die or you go on living – what is there to be afraid of in that? But I've always been so afraid – it's ridiculous, why should one be so afraid?'

The initial impassivity had now given way to a careless manner that was clearly the result of intoxication.

'And then,' he said, with a drunken toss of his head, 'and then you're even more afraid of what they'll say. You're a coward, they'll say, and that is worse than anything else. You're a coward. I'm not a coward. I don't want to be a coward. Actually, what would it matter if I were a coward? What would it matter if they said it, when I really am? But if I lose this job . . . I'll find another. They can always use you somewhere. They are damn well not going to throw me out. I'll go myself. Voluntarily, out of the Voluntary Sacrifice Service. Voluntarily, the way I came in.'

His face clouded over again, not so much unhappy as deeply bitter.

'I hate them,' he went on, suddenly hard-set. 'I hate them, strolling around their laboratories without flaw or blemish, not needing to be afraid of wounds or pain, or foreseen or unforeseen consequences. Then they go home to their wives and children. Do you think someone like me can have a family? I tried to get married once, but it didn't work out, I think you can understand that it didn't work out. You get too wrapped up in yourself when your life is like this. No woman can stand that. I hate all women. They entice you, you know, but then they can't stand you. They're deceitful. I hate them, except for my comrades in the Sacrifice Service, of course. The women in the Sacrifice Service aren't real women any more, they're nothing to hate. We who live over there, our life is not like that of others. We're called fellow soldiers too, but what sort of existence do we have? We must live in the Home, for we're like wrecks . . .'

His voice sank to an indistinct murmur, while he repeated: 'I hate . . .'

'My chief,' I said, 'do you want me to give him another injection?'

I hoped he would say no, as I found the man deeply unsympathetic. But Rissen nodded, and I had to obey. While I slowly released more pale-green liquid into No. 135's bloodstream, I said to him, quite sharply: 'Look, you yourself have quite rightly pointed out that it's called the *Voluntary* Sacrifice Service. Then what have you got to complain about? It's distasteful to hear a grown man complaining about his own actions. At some point you must have volunteered, without compulsion, you like all the rest.'

I am afraid that my words were not really addressed to the sedated man, who indeed in his sedation must have been quite unreceptive to reason, but rather to Rissen, so that at least he would know where he stood with me.

'Of course I went of my own accord,' mumbled No. 135, dazed and confused, 'of course I went of my own accord – but I didn't know that it was like it was. I think I thought it meant suffering – but in a different way, a more noble way – and dying – but instantly, and in rapture. Not day and night, inch by inch. I think it would be wonderful to die. You could beat your arms about. You could make the death rattle. I saw someone die at the Home once – he beat his arms about and rattled. It was dreadful. But it wasn't just dreadful. It can't be imitated. And ever since, I've never stopped thinking that it would be wonderful to be able to behave like that, just once. After all, we all have to do it, it's inevitable. If it was voluntary it would be indecent. But it isn't voluntary: no one is allowed to stop it for you. You simply do it. When you're dying you're allowed to behave any way you want, and no one can stop you.'

I stood twirling a glass rod in my fingers.

'The man must be perverse in some way,' I said to Rissen quietly. 'A healthy fellow soldier doesn't react like that.'

Rissen made no reply.

'Can you really be so inconsiderate as to put the blame . . .' I began a rather heated address to the test subject. I noticed that Rissen gave me a long look, at once cold and amused, and felt myself blushing at the notion that now he probably thought I was putting on airs for him. (A very unjust notion, I believed.) However, I had to finish the sentence, and continued in a rather more docile tone of voice: '. . . on others, because you've chosen a profession which now you don't think suits you?'

No. 135 did not appear to react at all to the tone and inflexion of my voice, merely to the question itself.

'Others?' he said. 'Me? But I don't want that. Though it's true, I did. There were ten of us from our section who signed up, more than from any other section in the whole youth camp. It passed through the camp like a hurricane – I've often wondered how that came about. Everything simply led to the Voluntary Sacrifice Service. Lectures, films, discussions: the Voluntary Sacrifice Service. And in the early years I still thought: it was worth all this. We went and signed up, you know. And when you looked at your neighbour, you didn't really see a human being any more. The faces, you see. Like fire. Not like flesh and blood. Sacred, divine. In the early years, I thought: it's been given to us to experience something different and greater than ordinary mortals experience, and now we are paying in, and we can, after what we have seen . . . But we can't. I can't. I can't hold on to the memory any more, it's slipping away, further and further away. Sometimes, before, it would gleam when I wasn't seeking it at all, but every time I seek – and I have to seek in order to find meaning in my life – I notice that it doesn't want to any more, it has slipped too far away. I think I've worn it out by seeking it too much. Sometimes I lie awake and brood about how it would have been if I'd had an ordinary life – would I have been able to experience a similarly great moment once more, perhaps, or perhaps not until now – or would all that greatness have spread out across my life, so that it still had a meaning – or at any rate, not have been so helplessly over, finished. Everyone needs a now, you know, not just a vanished moment that you must live on for the rest of your life. It's impossible to cope with this, even if you were once allowed to experience . . . But you're ashamed. Ashamed to betray the only moment in life that was worth something. Betray. Why does a person betray? All I want is an ordinary life, so I can find meaning again. I took on too much. I can't manage. Tomorrow I'll go and tell them that I'm quitting.'

A kind of relaxation ensued. Once more he broke the silence:

'Do you think you encounter a moment like that one more time – when you die? I've thought about that a lot. I would like to die. Even if you don't get anything from life any more, then at least you get that. When people say: I can't manage, they mean: I can't manage to live. They don't mean: I can't manage to die – for they can manage that, you can always manage to die, for then you can be as you want to be . . .'

He fell silent and sat still, leaning back in the chair. A greenish pallor began to spread across his face. His body jerked almost imperceptibly with light hiccups. His hands slid tentatively along the armrests, and the whole of the man seemed to waken to anxiety and nausea. Not surprising, incidentally, as he had had a double dose. I handed him a glass of water with drops of tranquillizer in it.

'He'll soon come to,' I said. 'As the effects wear off it's making him feel a bit unwell. Then it will be over. In one way he probably has the most unpleasant part of his work ahead of him: he must creep back into his fear and sense of shame. Look, my chief! I think it may be worth observing him.'

In fact, Rissen's eyes were already fixed on No. 135 with an expression that made it look as though it were he and not the test subject who was ashamed. The man before us really did not offer an encouraging spectacle. The veins at his temples bulged and swelled, and the muscles at the corners of his mouth quivered in suppressed horror of a much worse kind than the one he had concealed on his entrance to the room. He was keeping his eyes convulsively shut, as though hoping right up to the end that it would turn his all-too-clear memory into a bad dream.

'He remembers everything that's happened?' Rissen asked quietly.

'All of it, I'm afraid. Though I don't know whether it should be considered an advantage or a disadvantage.'

With extreme reluctance the test subject at last decided to open his eyes enough for him to be more or less able to feel his way forward across the floor. Stooped and uncertain, he took a few steps away from the chair without daring to look either of us in the face.

'Well, I thank you for your service,' I said, and sat down at the table. (Polite form required that the person addressed should then reply: 'I have only done my duty,' but not even a stickler for form such as I was in those days had the gall to adhere too strictly to convention when dealing with test subjects after the experiment.) 'I think I shall write the certificate immediately,' I said, 'so then you can get your fee from the cashier when you want. I shall file it under Class 8: moderate discomfort without subsequent injury. The pain and nausea are hardly worth mentioning, so it should really be Class 3. But I think I understand that you – hmm – how shall I put it – feel a little ashamed.'

Absentmindedly he picked up the document and hobbled on towards the door. There he stood for a few seconds in indecision, then all of a sudden turned round stiffly and stammered:

'Perhaps I should simply say that I don't know what came over me. It was as if I had taken leave of my senses and babbled things I didn't mean at all. No one could love their job more than I do, and quitting is naturally the last thing on my mind. I earnestly hope that I may demonstrate my good will by suffering the hardest experiments for the sake of the State.'

'I think you should at least stay until your hand has healed,' I said lightly. 'Otherwise you will probably find it hard to be accepted for any other job. Incidentally, what have you learned? As far as I know, they don't waste unnecessary extra training on a fellow soldier, and a man of your age won't normally be thrown into a new field of work, especially when one can't imagine any "invalid" status for the profession you have chosen . . .'

Even today I know that I spoke with haughty arrogance. The trouble was that I had unfortunately developed a marked dislike of my first test subject. I felt I had sufficient reasons for such an attitude: the cowardice and selfish irresponsibility that he concealed under a mask of bravery and willingness to sacrifice, when he was aware that his superiors wanted it to be that way. Yes, the guidelines of the Seventh Bureau had certainly got into my blood! As for the disguised cowardice, I could see for myself how repulsive it was, even though I failed to notice it when it was disguised sorrow. On the other hand, what I did not see clearly was another reason for my aversion, one that I only discovered and understood later: once again, envy. That man there, inferior as he was in many ways, spoke of a moment of lofty beatitude, already past and almost forgotten, but all the same, a moment ... His brief, ecstatic visit to the propaganda office at the youth camp on the day he signed up for the Voluntary Sacrifice Service – yes, I envied him that. Was it possible that one single moment of that kind would have slaked my unquenchable thirst, the thirst I vainly sought to slake with Linda? Though I did not think these thoughts through to the end, I had a feeling that the man was a recipient of special grace, but an ungrateful one, and that made me hard.

Instead, Rissen behaved in a way that struck me with astonishment. He went straight up to No. 135, put a hand on his shoulder and said in a tone so warm that one hardly ever heard it used with adults, least of all among men, but at most when particularly emotional mothers spoke to young children:

'Don't be afraid now. You must understand that nothing personal will get out here. It's as if it had never been said.'

The man looked up shyly, turned round in haste and vanished through the doorway. I thought I understood his embarrassment. Had he had an ounce more pride, I thought, he would surely have spat in the face of a chief who took such a familiar bearing with a subordinate. And I also thought: how can one respect and obey a chief like that? The person of whom no one needs to be afraid can demand no respect either, naturally enough, as respect always contains an acknowledgement of strength, superiority, power – and strength, superiority and power are always dangerous to those around them.

So we were alone, Rissen and I, and a long silence fell over the room. I did not like Rissen's pauses. They were neither rest nor work, they formed an approximation.

'I know what you're thinking, my chief,' I said at last, to get the conversation going. 'You're thinking that this doesn't prove anything. I might have instructed the man beforehand. What he said was certainly compromising on a personal level, but not punishable. That's what you're thinking, isn't it?'

'No,' said Rissen, looking as though he were waking up. 'No, I wasn't thinking that. I suppose it was clear enough that the man said some things that he really meant, but would never normally have said out loud for the life of him. There can be no doubt that it was genuine, both what he confessed and his shame afterwards.'

I suppose that in my own interest I have should have been glad of his credulity, but the fact was that it irritated me, as I thought it too flippant. In our World State, where every fellow soldier is brought up from his earliest years to exercise strict self-control, it would certainly not have been impossible that No. 135 had staged a magnificent theatrical performance, though at present this happened not to be the case. But I kept my criticism to myself, and merely replied:

'Is it undisciplined if I suggest that we continue?'

The strange man did not seem to notice what I said.

'A singular discovery,' he said, reflectively. 'How did you come to make it?'

'I built on previous research,' I answered. 'A drug with similar effects has been in existence for nearly five years, but it has such toxic side effects that, almost without exception, the test subjects ended up in a mental hospital – even if they used the drug only once. The researcher killed a large number of people with it, and he was given a sharp warning to put the whole thing aside. Now I have succeeded in neutralizing the toxic side effects. I must admit that I was very concerned about how it would work in practice . . .'

And quickly, almost more in passing, I added:

'I hope that my discovery will be named Kallocain, after me.'

'No doubt, no doubt,' said Rissen, indifferently. 'Do you yourself have an idea of the importance it will have?'

'Yes, I think I do. When need is greatest, help is nearest, as they say. You know that the courts are starting to overflow with false evidence. There is hardly a trial where the statements of the various witnesses don't contradict one another, and in a way that can't possibly be caused by mistakes or negligence. What really causes it no one is able to determine, but it is so.'

'Is it so hard?' asked Rissen, drumming his fingers on the edge of the table in a way that irritated me. 'Is it really so hard to determine it? Allow me to ask a question – well, you don't need to answer it, if you don't want to – but do you consider perjury wrong under all circumstances?'

'Of course not,' I replied, in slight annoyance. 'Not if the State's welfare demands it. But one can't say that about every little trivial case.'

'Yes, but just think about it,' said Rissen slyly, putting his head on one side. 'Is it not in the State's best interest if a villain is convicted, even though he may be innocent of the particular crime with which he is charged? Is it not in the State's best interest if my good-for-nothing, harmful, extremely unsympathetic enemy is convicted, even though he hasn't really done anything punishable according to the law? *He'll* demand consideration, of course, but what right to consideration does the individual have . . .'

I could not really see where he was heading, and time was passing. Quickly I rang for the next test subject myself, and while I was injecting her, I replied:

'Anyway, all that has turned out to be a lot of mischief, and of no benefit to the State whatsoever, quite the reverse. But my discovery will solve that problem overnight. Not only will the witnesses now be able to be verified – they won't even be needed, as the criminal will confess, gladly and without reservation, after a small injection. We know about the inconveniences of the third degree – yes, don't misunderstand me, I'm not criticizing the fact that it's been used, of course, in the absence of any other method – after all, one can't very well go around feeling solidarity with criminals, when one knows one has nothing on one's conscience . . .'

'You seem to have an unusually solid conscience,' said Rissen, drily. 'Or are you merely pretending? Actually, in my experience no fellow soldier over forty has a really clear conscience. Some do, when they're young perhaps, but later . . . I say, perhaps you're not over forty yet, are you?'

'No, I'm not,' I replied as calmly as I could. Luckily I was turned towards the new test subject and could thus avoid looking at Rissen face to face. I was upset, but not principally because of his insolence to me. What irritated me much more was the general trend of his assertions. What an intolerable situation he painted – where all fellow soldiers who reached the age of maturity had a chronically bad conscience! Although he did not say it straight out, I dimly felt it as an attack on the values I held most sacred.

He must have noticed the dismissiveness in my tone, and realized he had gone too far. We worked on, without saying any more than was completely necessary and to the point.

When I endeavour to recall the experiments that followed, they definitely turn out to lack the same clear contours and the same colour and life as the first one. The first experiment had of course been the most exciting one, but I still could not feel entirely sure that my drug would *always* prove effective, even though it had worked well on the first occasion. I suspect that what disturbed me was my indignation at Rissen. However painstakingly I worked, it was only with half my attention, and perhaps for that reason this work did not strike such deep roots in my memory as the first experiment had done. I shall therefore not bother to try to describe all the details. It is enough if I can record the general impression.

Since by lunchtime we had already dealt with the five test subjects who had been sent down to us, and another two besides, each more bandaged and wretched than the last, I felt completely bruised and battered, and full of a growing contempt mixed with horror. Was it really only the riff-raff who applied to the Voluntary Sacrifice Service, I wondered. But I knew full well that it was not. I knew that highly estimable qualities were needed for someone to apply there, that courage, readiness to make a sacrifice, self-effacement and determination were required before one committed oneself to such a profession. Neither would I nor could I imagine that the profession destroyed those who had chosen it. But the insights I obtained into the private lives of the test subjects were depressing.

No. 135 had been cowardly and hidden his cowardice. At

least in keeping the great moment in his life sacred he had
shown an attractive side of his nature. The others were as cowardly as he, some even rather more so. There were those who
only complained, not just about their calling – the wounds, the
illnesses and the fear that were their self-chosen lot – but also
about a large number of trivial matters: the beds at the Home,
the deterioration in the quality of the food (so they had also
noticed it!), the negligence in health care. One might have
thought that there had been a great moment in their lives, too,
but if so it had already sunk out of reach. Perhaps they had not
exerted such a large amount of willpower as 135 had done in
order to keep it intact. To tell the truth: no matter how unheroic
No. 135 had seemed as he sat there in his Kallocain intoxication, when I compared him with the others he actually began to
strike me as a relative hero. But there were also a great many
other things that disgusted and frightened me in the test subjects we used during the initial period: more or less developed
oddities, macabre fantasies, surreptitious lechery. Then there
were some who did not avail themselves of the Home, but were
married and had their own apartments; they exposed their
marital problems in a manner that was both pathetic and laughable. To put it briefly: one must either despair of the Voluntary
Sacrifice Service, or of all the fellow soldiers in the World State,
or of the biological species of man in general.

And to each and every one of them Rissen made the same
solemn promise that their precious secrets were now in safe
keeping. This I found hard to swallow.

After one particularly bad case – on the first day, moreover,
it was our last case before lunch – an old man who fantasized
about sex murder, though he had clearly never done anything
of the kind and would probably never have a chance to, I could
not help giving free rein to my painful mood, and turned to
Rissen with a quite unmotivated apology for my test subjects.

'You really think they are such uniquely rotten apples?'

'It's true that they're not all sex murderers in the making,'
I replied, 'but they all seem to be more wretched than is
permissible.'

I had expected him to agree. It would have brought me relief

and to some extent removed me a little from the whole embarrassing situation. When I noticed that he did not share my
strong abhorrence, it all became twice as embarrassing. Yet as
we walked up to the refectory we continued the conversation.

'Permissible, yes, permissible,' said Rissen. Then he switched
to a different tone and line of thought, and continued: 'Be
thankful that we haven't had any saints and heroes of the permissible kind – I suspect I would have felt less convinced then.
Actually, we haven't encountered a single real criminal either.'

'Yes, but this last one, this last one! I admit he has done nothing wrong, and I don't think he will commit any of the misdeeds
he fantasizes about, old as he is and in the care of the Home,
where I'm sure there is nothing wrong with the supervision. But
imagine if he were young and had the opportunity of putting
his desires into action! In cases like that my Kallocain will be a
good thing to have. With it, we'll be able to predict and prevent
many monstrous deeds that at present are committed before
anyone can count to three or see them coming . . .'

'Provided you get hold of the right people. That's not so
easy, either. For you don't really mean that everyone should be
investigated?'

'Why not? Why not everyone? I know it's a dream of the future,
but even so I foresee a time when all appointments to official
posts will be preceded by a Kallocain test, just as naturally as
they are now preceded by the usual psycho-technical tests. That
way not only the registrant's professional qualifications but also
his or her value as a fellow soldier will be public knowledge. I
would even go so far as to fantasize about an obligatory annual
Kallocain examination of every fellow soldier . . .'

'Your plans for the future are not exactly small ones,' Rissen
broke in. 'But there would be too much bureaucracy.'

'You're quite right, my chief, there would be too much bureaucracy. It would need a whole new government department,
with hordes of employees who would all have to be drawn
from the now established production and military organization. Before such a new order is established, we would clearly
need to have the increase in population for which we have
campaigned for so many years but have not yet seen any sign

of. Perhaps we can hope for another great war of conquest that will make us richer and more productive.'

But Rissen shook his head.

'Oh, of course not,' he said. 'As soon as they discover that your plan is the most necessary of all, the only necessary one, the only one that can allay our overwhelming – yes, let us say overwhelming – concerns, you may be certain that this department of yours will come into being. It will come into being – we shall have to wind down our standard of living, we shall have to increase our tempo of labour, and the great, beautiful sense of complete security and certainty will have to replace what we lose.'

I was unsure whether he was being serious or whether this was intended as some kind of irony. On the one hand, I was ready to heave a sigh at the thought of an even more reduced standard of living. (One is so ungrateful, I thought, one is self-indulgent and selfish, even when it's a matter of things that are greater than the individual's satisfaction.) On the other hand, I felt flattered by the thought that one day Kallocain would play such a role. But before I could make any reply at all, he added in a different tone:

'We may be rather sure of one thing – the last remnants of our private lives are now gone.'

'Oh well, *that* doesn't matter so much!' I said cheerfully. 'The collective stands ready to conquer the last area where asocial tendencies could previously take refuge. As far as I can see, it means quite simply that the great community is near completion.'

'The community,' he repeated slowly, as if he had doubts about it.

I did not have time to reply. We were standing inside the refectory doorway, and had to part company in order to go to our places at different tables. To stop and finish our conversation was impossible, partly because it would have caused surprise, and partly because we could not stand in the way of the enormous stream of people who were yearning for their lunch. But while I went to my place and sat down, I thought about his doubtful tone, and felt annoyed.

After all, he must have known what I meant; it was not a

free invention of mine, what I had said about the community. From childhood onwards, every fellow soldier had to learn the difference between the lower and the higher forms of life: the lower form uncomplicated and undifferentiated – for example, the monocellular creatures and plants – the higher form complex, with multifaceted differentiation, for example, the human body in its refined and well-functioning composition. Each fellow soldier also had to learn that it was exactly the same with the forms of society: from an aimless horde the societal body had developed into the most highly organized and differentiated of all forms: our present World State. From individualism to collectivism – from isolation to community, that was the path that had been followed by this gigantic and sacred organism in which the individual was merely a cell with no other significance than to serve the organism as a whole. That much was known by every young person who had attended the children's camp, and that much Rissen also ought to know. Moreover, he ought to have understood something that was not so difficult to understand: that Kallocain was a necessary step in the whole of this development, as it expanded the community to the inner realm that people had hitherto kept to themselves. Did Rissen really not understand something that was so logical – or did he not want to understand?

I glanced at his table. There he sat with his slouching posture, stirring his soup with a distracted look. The whole of the man disturbed me in a vague sort of way. He was not only peculiar in the sense of being unlike others to the point of absurdity; he was also peculiar in another way, where I had a hazy apprehension of danger. As yet I did not know what this danger might be, but it drew my reluctant attention to all that he said and did.

Our experiments were to continue after lunch, and now a more complex investigation awaited. I had planned it with a more sceptical control chief in mind than Rissen, but in any case precision was a virtue. After all, my experiments would not remain with Rissen; if he approved them, they would be discussed in many circles in the chemistry cities, perhaps even among the lawyers in the capital. The test subjects we sent for now did not need to be fresh, that was the special instruction; as long as they had the full use of their senses that was enough. On the other hand, they had to fulfil another condition, one that was doubtless extremely seldom required of a commissioned test subject: they had to be married.

We had called up the chief of police on the phone to obtain permission for this new experiment. Even though we controlled the Voluntary Sacrifice Service's employees, body and soul, with no other motive than the State's best interests, we did not have similar power over their wives and husbands, any more than we did over other fellow soldiers. For that we had to have the police chief's special consent. Initially he was slightly reluctant, thought it unnecessary, as long as there were professional sacrifice servants, and did not really see what all the fuss was about. But once we had worked on him for long enough, so that he grew impatient amid all his haste and bustle, and once we had convinced him that nothing worse would happen to the subjects than fear and mild nausea, he at last gave his permission. However, he told us to come and see him in the evening to give him more precise information in more peaceful surroundings.

The ten married sacrifice servants were called in one by one. In my card system I had not only to enter their numbers, but also their names and addresses, which did not appear at all on their cards, and that also caused a certain amount of consternation and alarm. I had to calm them down and brief them on what lay ahead.

The plan was that they should come home to their husband or wife showing signs of concern and anxiety, or, if they found it easier, a certain rosy optimism about the future. Finally, when pressed, they were to say in confidence that they had engaged in an act of espionage. Perhaps on the metro a neighbour had whispered in their ear that they could earn a lot of money by simply drawing a map of the laboratories around the central office of the Voluntary Sacrifice Service – the laboratories and the metro lines, as they imagined them, more or less. Then they simply had to wait and not let their expression betray the fact that it was an experiment.

That same evening we went to police headquarters, duly

equipped with a certificate from the most senior official in our laboratory district, and a visitors' permit from police headquarters sent by express courier. I had narrowly succeeded in exchanging my evening of military and police duty for a double spell of duty later on. We were, however, glad to make contact with the chief of police; we needed his help in what we now planned to do. In fact it was a rather onerous task to convince him, not because he had any general difficulty in understanding, but because he was in a bad mood, and clearly viewed everyone with distrust on principle. I must confess that his distrust made a better impression on me than Rissen's credulousness. Even though it happened to be at my expense, it was perfectly normal, and when we finally got him over to our side I at least had the feeling that I had opened a very secure door with the right and lawful key, not with a jemmy and not with a kick.

The important thing was that we had to get hold of the male or female partners of the people who were our test subjects, since they had gained the confidence of their partners. They could of course be denounced in the legal manner, as accessories to conspiracy, and be arrested in accordance with all the tricks of the trade, as long as they were then delivered to us in some way. If the chief of police wanted to let his men know the details of the case or preferred to keep the knowledge to himself, that was his private concern. All that mattered was that the arrested partners should be Kallocain-tested by us. If he wished, he could check for himself that these remand prisoners came to no harm in our care, and thus that no human material was needlessly destroyed – if he wanted to come in person or send a representative, that was equally acceptable and we would feel flattered. In point of fact, I think it was this mention of 'in person' that improved his mood. Despite his ill humour, he was curious to see how my discovery might work. When we finally received the written confirmation of his earlier telephoned promise, with the signature 'Vay Karrek' in tall, pointed but vigorous handwriting at the bottom, we prepared him for the risk that some of the unsuspecting partners might make up their minds to denounce the pretended criminals. Of course, since the whole thing was a game it ought not to lead to any legal proceedings – we handed him the list of the test subjects' names – but we would naturally be grateful if the partners were arrested as early as possible the following morning.

Tired but happy with the result of our trip, we returned from police headquarters.

When I got home and into the parents' room – Linda had already gone to bed – a message awaited me on the bedside table. It concerned my military and police duty: from four evenings a week it was being increased to five. For the time being, therefore, the authorities felt compelled to reduce the family evenings from two to one, while the evening of celebration and speeches was retained uncurtailed. (The latter was also necessary not only for the fellow soldiers' recreation and nurture, but also for the perpetuation of the State. Where and when else would fellow soldiers who had already left the youth camp meet one another and fall in love? Linda and I also had those evenings of celebrations and speeches to thank for our marriage.) This was a message wholly in keeping with the signs I had earlier observed, and I saw that a similar document addressed to Linda lay on the table.

The family evenings were usually interrupted by all sorts of issues; I knew that from experience. If things went badly, it might be a long time until I had an evening to myself. As it was not yet particularly late and I was not as tired as one generally is after evening spells of duty, I decided to lose no time in doing what had to happen, so I sat down and wrote the apology I was going to ask to be broadcast on the radio:

'I, Leo Kall, employed at the 4th Chemistry City's central laboratory for anaesthetics and organic poisons, experimental department, have an apology to make.

'At the youth camp farewell banquet for conscripted employees on April 19 this year I committed a serious error. Affected with a false compassion, of the kind that results from sympathy with the individual, and a false heroism, of a type that dwells with predilection on the dark and tragic instead of the light and cheerful things in life, I gave the following speech.' (Here the speech was interpolated, and it was to be read in a lightly ironic tone.) 'Now the Seventh Bureau of the Ministry of Propaganda has issued the following statement about this speech: "When a wholehearted ...", etc.' (The statement would also be repeated, as it was after all the most important item for the listeners, setting a legal precedent and a warning for all who shared the same paths of thought and feeling.) 'I herewith tender my apology for my regrettable error and perceive how deeply and completely justified is the Seventh Bureau's displeasure, just as I feel in my innermost being a willingness to be guided henceforth by its very convincing appraisal of the matter.'

Next morning I asked Linda to read the text through quickly, and she thought it would do. It was in no way exaggerated, no one could read into it any secret irony, while at the same time no one could accuse it of any stupid, false pride. So all that remained was to make a fair copy, send it in, and then stand in line to await my turn on the radio's apology hour.

CHAPTER 5

The experiment immediately took a rather ominous turn. Very early in the morning we telephoned police headquarters to hear if anything had happened, and yet we were clearly still too late. In no less than nine cases out of ten, the partners had denounced their spouses. Whether the tenth subject might perhaps also be on the way to doing so, it was hard to tell – at any rate an arrest warrant had been issued, and we could expect the subject in question to be at our laboratory within two or three hours.

Not exactly a brilliant outlook. I must admit I was a little surprised at how loyal, for the most part, and how quick to change their attitude, all these partners had shown themselves to be – most gratifying, of course, had it not been for the demands of the experiment. It was certain that the test would have to be repeated. We would have to be able to present at least one or two verified cases before the discovery could be used by the State.

We therefore sent for a new group of ten married test subjects, and I repeated my little speech of the previous day. Everything took precisely the same course, with the only difference that this time they were all in even worse shape – one or two even arrived hopping on crutches, and one had the whole of his head in bandages. It might well be that married test subjects were few, and in this particular experiment the crutches were of no significance at all – but even so! Of late the shortage of subjects had become ever more perceptible. They had obviously been used up with the passage of the years, and something would have to be done if the work was to be continued as before. As soon as the subjects had left the room, I burst out:

'But it's a scandal! Soon we shall run out of personnel altogether! We'll have to experiment on people who are dying and mentally deranged! Isn't it time the authorities got a campaign going again, the kind of campaign our first test subject was talking about, to replenish the thinning ranks?'

'There is nothing to prevent you from complaining,' said Rissen, with a shrug of his shoulders.

I had an idea. Of course, and rightly so, the authorities would attach no importance to a complaint written by an individual fellow soldier. On the other hand, one could very well start a petition, with the gathering of names from all the city's laboratories where test subjects were used and where the shortage must have been observed. I decided to use the first evening when I was not too tired, in the worst case one of my evenings off, to formulate such a text, which could then be duplicated and circulated around the various institutes. Initiatives of this kind could not possibly be anything but meritorious, I thought.

The hours before the prisoner on remand arrived were devoted to a kind of inquiry that Rissen set up, concerning Kallocain and its closer relatives among pharmaceuticals, viewed from a chemical and medicinal standpoint. He was skilful in his area of expertise – that I could not deny. I think I managed it all rather well, and I was surprised that he considered me worthy of such an inquiry. Was it his intention to declare me qualified for some higher position? From a purely objective point of view, I surely was, and yet . . . It seemed to me that he must have felt my distrust like gooseflesh on his skin, and he replied in the same coin. With strong inner reservations I accepted his friendliness. What he might hope or need from me in future it was impossible to guess. At all events, I did not plan to allow myself to be lulled into a false sense of security.

When the appointed time drew near, a man in police uniform came in and announced the arrival of Police Chief Karrek himself. He must be really interested, then! It was of course an honour for the whole institute, but especially for me, that such a powerful man should attend my experiment. With a somewhat ironic look – he himself probably thought he was displaying his curiosity too freely – he sat down in the chair we provided for him. A short time later the remand prisoner was led in, a rather young, frail and slightly haggard little woman. Either she was pale-skinned from birth, or her facial pallor was caused by tension.

'You have sent in a denunciation to the police?' I asked, to be on the safe side.

'No,' she said in astonishment, and became a shade more transparent. (She could not possibly have been any paler.)

'And you have nothing to confess, either?' asked Rissen.

'No!' (Now her voice was perfectly steady again, without any note of surprise.)

'You are accused of involvement in treason. Think carefully, now: has anyone close to you mentioned anything about treasonous conspiracies?'

'No!' she replied, very firmly.

I heaved a sigh of relief. Either from criminality or from pure laziness she had failed to denounce her husband in time – *now*, at any rate, she was in no mood to confess. She was probably afraid. In normal circumstances her strict posture and hard-set look would have suggested a bold and energetic fellow soldier. Now they made her seem defiant and rebellious. I almost smiled when I thought of the artful illusion she was hiding like a precious secret, and of how we were going to force it out of her – we, who knew what it was worth . . . Even more, when one thought of how much pointless trouble she had already experienced, transported at express speed in a sealed carriage on the metro's deepest branch, the police and military line, being gagged and put in handcuffs, and guarded by two policemen – customary when a traitor was being taken somewhere. But my smile never met the daylight. Even though the story was a fabrication and the whole investigation a comedy – her involvement was real enough, and just as criminal whether it stemmed from evil intent or from laziness.

When she was seated on the chair she was close to fainting. She probably thought my innocent laboratory was a torture chamber where we were now going to force out of her what she did not want to say. While Rissen dealt with her fainting, I gave her an injection, and in silence all three of us waited – the police chief, Rissen and I.

From this frail and frightened test subject, who was not even a professional but only an amateur, if one may use such a partisan expression, anyone might have expected a tearful reaction like that of No. 135, my first victim. But it was rather the reverse. The stiff and tensed features relaxed slowly, infinitely slowly, into an inward-turned, childlike clarity. The lines on the heavy forehead were erased. Surprisingly enough, over the thin cheeks, the prominent cheekbones, slid an almost happy smile. With a jerk she sat up straight in the chair, opened her eyes wide and drew a deep breath. For a long time she sat in silence, until I began to fear that my Kallocain might yet in the end prove unreliable.

'No, there is nothing to be afraid of, is there,' she said at last, in a wondering tone of relief. 'He must know it, too. Not pain, not death. Not anything. He knows it. Why should I not say it? Why should I not talk about this, too? Yes of course, he told me about it, last night he talked about it – and now I realize that he probably already knew what I didn't know until now: that there's nothing to be afraid of. But the fact that he knew it, when he talked to me, I shall never forget that. That he dared. I would never have dared. But it's the pride of my life that he dared, and I shall be grateful all my life, I shall live in gratitude, to do the same in return.'

'What was it he dared?' I broke in, eager to get to the point.

'To talk to me. About something I would not have dared . . .'

'And what did he talk about, then?'

'It doesn't matter. It has no meaning. Something stupid. Someone who wanted him to give them information, sketch-maps, and pay him money for it. He hasn't done it yet. He said he was thinking of doing it, but I don't understand it. I would never do it. But he wanted to talk to me about it – I want to talk to him again. Either he will come to understand me, or I will also come to understand him. We will understand each other and act together when we act. I am with him. With him, I have nothing to fear. He was not afraid of me.'

'Sketch-maps? But don't you know that all attempts to make

maps of any kind are strictly forbidden and are considered treason?'

'Yes – yes, of course I know that – I told you, I don't understand him,' she replied impatiently. 'But we shall understand each other. I him or he me. Then we shall act together. Don't you see: I've been afraid of him. And he was not afraid of me. Because he talked about this. And he has no reason, either. He will never have any reason. Never. I realized it was because I had . . .'

'So,' I interrupted with a violence for which I really had no grounds, 'so: he had agreed to sell sketch-maps to someone. What sort of sketch-maps?'

'Maps of the laboratories,' she replied, indifferently. 'But I realized it was because I had . . .'

'And you knew it was treason? And that by not denouncing him you were making yourself an accessory to treason?'

'Yes, yes. But the other thing was more important . . .'

'Do you know anything about the man who wanted the sketch-maps?'

'Well, I asked him, but he didn't know much himself. The man sat beside him on the metro and said he would appear again, but wouldn't say where and when, just that he would pay when he got the sketches. Before then, we had to come to an agreement . . .'

'It's enough, what we have here,' I said, turning half to Rissen and half to the police chief. 'We've succeeded in getting out of her all the information the husband had been tasked with delivering. The rest of it is just trivial stuff.'

'This is truly interesting,' said the police chief. 'Extremely interesting. Can one really make people so outspoken by such simple means? But you must forgive me, I'm a sceptic by nature. Of course I have complete trust in your good faith and conscientiousness, complete trust. And yet I would like to watch this a few more times. Don't misunderstand me, Fellow Soldiers. It makes perfect sense that the police are interested in your discovery.'

With the greatest of pleasure we told him that he was welcome to visit whenever he liked, and at the same time took care to give him the list of the new test subjects. Hopefully this group would not come to grief like the first one, I thought. Hardly had the thought entered my mind than I was transfixed with horror: here I was, wishing a certain number of subjects to be traitorously inclined fellow soldiers ... Rissen's words from the day before came back to me: no fellow soldier over forty had a clear conscience. And at once I found myself seething with violent resentment towards Rissen, as though it were he that had forced me into the treasonous wish. Perhaps in a way I was right – not that my desire was his work, but that without his words this antagonism might never have occurred to me.

The woman in the chair stirred, with a whimper, and Rissen gave her the camphor bottle.

Suddenly she leapt up with a scream. She crouched in horror, put her hands to her mouth and began to wail loudly; she had reached the point where she had full use of her senses again, and saw what she had done.

It was a terrible and sorry sight, but it also filled me with a certain satisfaction. A few moments ago, as she sat there in childlike insouciance, I had breathed more deeply and calmly than usual, against my will. She emanated a kind of repose that to me recalled sleep – though I must say I don't think I fall into a repose like that when I am asleep, and much less so when waking. There she had sat, believing herself to be at ease with another person, her husband – and he had already betrayed her, he had betrayed her from the outset – and now she had also betrayed him without meaning to. Unreal as his crime had been, so also her sense of security just then had been unreal, unreal as her terror now. I found myself thinking of the Fata Morgana that the desert wanderer sees above the salt flats: palm trees, oases, springs – if the worst comes to the worst, he leans down, drinks from the salty pools and perishes. That was what she had done, I thought, and such always is the potion that we lap up from asocial, individualistic-sentimental sources. An illusion, a dangerous illusion.

It struck me that she ought to be told the whole truth, not so that she could escape her wild contrition, but so that she would perceive the whole emptiness of the brief sense of security she had had.

'Calm yourself,' I said. 'You have no reason to complain, at least not for your husband's sake. Take heed of what I say: *your husband has never met that man.* Your husband is completely innocent. That whole story was something we instructed him to tell you. It was an experiment – with you!'

She stared at me, seemingly unable to take this in.

'The whole spy story was made up,' I repeated, unable to repress a smile, though I did not really think there was anything to smile about. 'Your husband's confession yesterday was nothing of the kind. He was acting on orders.'

For a moment it looked as though she was about to faint again, but then she stiffened and straightened up. There she stood, thin and petrified, in the middle of the floor, without taking a step forward or back. I had nothing more to say to her, but could not take my eyes off her. As she stood there now, closed and rigid like a dead thing, without a drop left of her recent happy sense of security, she aroused a violent compassion in me. It was a weakness to be ashamed of, but it was too powerful for me. I forgot the police chief, I forgot Rissen, and I was engulfed by a vague desire to make her understand that I felt as she did now ... From this painful second of torpor I awoke when the police chief said:

'I think the woman should continue to be held in detention. It is true that the treason itself was make-believe, but her participation in it was as real as it could be. On the other hand, we cannot simply pass judgement off the cuff, and it will have to be dealt with in a slightly more lawful fashion.'

'Impossible!' cried Rissen, bewildered. 'Remember that it's an experiment, it involves our employees, or more strictly their spouses . . .'

'How could I take that into account?' asked Karrek, laughing.

For once I was completely on Rissen's side.

'A detention of that kind would undoubtedly become public knowledge,' I said, 'even if we were to dismiss her husband and transfer him somewhere else – which is hard enough to do with sacrifice servants, in poor health as they are – even then the story would get out, and the recruitment figures within the profession, which are already so low, would probably fall to disastrous levels. I beg you, for the sake of the whole case, forget about the detention!'

'You exaggerate,' replied Karrek. 'The story doesn't need to get out. Why should her husband be transferred somewhere else? He could very easily have an accident on his way home.'

'It cannot be your intention to take from us one of our few and precious test subjects,' I replied in a querulous tone. 'As far as the woman is concerned, she is no longer dangerous: on another occasion she will not accept confidences so lightly. Actually,' I added on a sudden impulse, 'if you detain our test subject it will mean that you have already made Kallocain a lawful means of interrogation, and you yourself expressed the view that it was too early to do so, my chief . . .'

The police chief narrowed his eyes to small slits, smiled pointedly yet kindly, and said as if he were addressing a child:

'By the look of it, you have the gift of speech and logic. For the laboratory's sake I shall yield in the matter of the detention, though it gives me no personal satisfaction to do so. I must go now –' he glanced at his watch – 'but I will return to see more experiments.'

He left, and the woman was freed from her handcuffs and allowed to go. Both for the laboratory's sake and for hers I breathed a sigh of relief. As she was being led out she walked stiffly, like a sleepwalker, and for the second time she sent a dreadful thought passing through my brain: what if I had miscalculated, what if my Kallocain turned out to have the same negative after-effects as its predecessors, perhaps not always, but on particularly sensitive nervous systems? But I calmed myself, and none of my apprehensions were realized. Through her husband I later found out that she seemed completely normal, if somewhat more reserved than before. 'Though she has always been reserved,' he added.

When we were alone again, Rissen said:

'We had the seeds of another kind of community there.'

'Community?' I asked, astonished. 'What do you mean?'

'With her, the woman.'

'Oh!' I said, ever more surprised. 'But that sort of community – yes, you are right, my chief, one may perhaps call it the seeds of community – but no more than that! That sort of community existed back in the Stone Age! In our day it's a sign of imperfect development, and a harmful one. Isn't it so?'

'Hmm,' was all he said.

'But this incident was really just a textbook example of where it may lead if individuals are too firmly bonded to each other!' I said, pleading my case emotionally. 'Then the most important bond of all, the bond to the State, may easily be broken!'

'Hmm,' he said again. And a moment later: 'Perhaps life in the Stone Age was not so bad after all.'

'A matter of taste, of course. If one prefers the struggle of all against all to the well-organized State built on mutual assistance – then life in the Stone Age must have been very agreeable. It's really amusing to think there are Neanderthals in our midst . . .'

I had meant him, but lost my nerve as I said it, and added: 'I mean that woman, naturally.'

He seemed to turn away, so as not to show that he was smiling. Awkward, what can slip out of one, quite without Kallocain, I thought.

CHAPTER 6

When I came home after the end of the working day the concierge told me that someone had asked for a temporary surface permit in the laboratory district, to be able to meet me in person. I stared at the name. Kadidja Kappori. No one I knew. At least, I could not recall having heard the name before. The concierge had not been able to determine on the telephone the precise reason for this woman's visit; he thought it concerned a divorce. Extremely strange! In the end I was so curious that I threw caution to the winds and signed the document which said that I was willing to receive her and when I would be able to do so. I saw to it that the concierge also signed, that he was party to the invitation and would control the time for the visit; then all that remained was to deliver the request to the district controller, who would write out the visitor's permit and send it to the registrant.

So then Linda and I bolted down our evening meal and each set off to do our respective military duty. It turned out to have been expanded, not only quantitively, but also qualitatively. During the days that immediately followed I came to view my working hours as the least demanding part of the day, while my most urgent task was the evening spell of duty, which often stretched into the night. I was glad that my discovery was complete. Had I been just a little slower, it might never have reached completion, at least if my evenings had always continued to be as they were now. With such hours of exertion behind me I would have sought in vain to gather my thoughts in full focus. Now it was merely a question of the final practical application, and it was progressing at full speed, particularly as Rissen's presence kept me awake. It was noticeable that he, too, was rather tired, but as he was somewhat older, his training drill was likely somewhat less harsh, and at any rate I never caught him making a mistake.

However, simply because of all the denunciations, the experiments appeared to have got stuck in the doldrums. We had to redo them, batch by batch, and meanwhile continue with the same tests we had carried out on the first day.

When we had redone our tests for the third time without a single husband or wife having delayed their denunciations long enough for them to be arrested – and what a labour it was getting married test subjects together, it cannot be described, the last time we had to wait three days before we gathered enough of them – my one night off of the week finally arrived, and no pleasure could have lured me more seductively than the thought of being able to go to bed a few hours earlier than what is usually meant by bedtime. The children were already asleep, the home help had left, I had set the alarm clock and was stretching for one last time.

Kadidja Kappori! I thought at once, cursing the submissiveness that had made me sign that senseless request for a visit. The worst of it was that on top of everything else I was on my own. Linda had had to use her free evening for a committee meeting being held to prepare a celebration for the director of the city's food factories, who was now retiring, and for the new director who was to replace her.

When I opened the door, an ageing woman stood outside, large and coarse, with a face that was none too intelligent.

'Fellow Soldier Leo Kall?' she asked. 'I am Kadidja Kappori, and it's very kind of you to have granted me an interview.'

'I am very sorry, but I happen to be at home alone,' I said, 'and therefore cannot be at your service. My regrets if you have travelled a long way to get here this evening, but you will be aware that there have been various provocations in which the accused have found it extremely difficult to prove their innocence because there were no witnesses and on those occasions the police didn't have that particular room under surveillance . . .'

'But nothing like that is involved,' she said, imploringly. 'I assure you that I come with the best of intentions.'

'I don't mistrust you personally, of course,' I replied, 'but you must admit that anyone can say that. At any rate, the safest thing for me is not to let you in. I don't know you, and no one knows what you might say about me afterwards.'

All this time I had been speaking in a rather loud voice in order to emphasize my innocence to the neighbours. It must have been this that gave her an idea.

'Maybe you could possibly invite some of your neighbours in as witnesses?' she asked. 'Though I have to admit that I'd rather talk to you alone.'

Undeniably a solution. I rang at the nearest door. A staff doctor at the experimental laboratories' refectories lived there; all I really knew about him was what he looked like, and that he and his wife sometimes quarrelled a bit too loudly for the thin dividing walls in the apartment building. When I rang his doorbell, he himself came to the door with raised eyebrows, and I declared my errand. His eyebrows slowly settled, he began to look interested, and finally gave his consent. He too was at home alone. For a moment I thought the better of it and wondered if this was the right thing to do, but there was really no reason to suppose that he was in some kind of conspiracy with Kadidja Kappori.

So they both came into the parents' room, where I hastily folded the already made bed into the wall to make slightly more room and give the place more of the atmosphere of a living room.

'You don't know who I am, of course,' she began. 'I am married to Togo Bahara of the Voluntary Sacrifice Service.'

My heart sank, though I tried to restrain my hostility. So she was one of the loyal fellow soldiers who had ruined my experiment. She had probably come here to denounce her husband. Why she was turning to me instead of going straight to the police, I really had no idea. Perhaps she detected something suspicious? Or perhaps she thought it less brutal to denounce him to his chief. Either way I could not possibly stop her now I had let her in, and the doctor was there as a witness.

'Something dreadfully sad has happened at home,' she continued, with her eyes lowered. 'The other day my husband came home and told me about something awful, the most awful thing of all, treason. I couldn't believe my ears. For over twenty years we've stuck together, brought several children into the world, so I always thought I knew him. I've had my spells of nervous irritation and depression, but that's just part of the job, of course. Actually, I work as a laundress at the Central Laundry in the laboratory district, and that's also where we were given our apartment. Though it's not strictly relevant to this. But you see, I thought I knew him. Not because we've ever talked to one another that much, when you've been married for a few years you know more or less what you have to say, and then you might just as well leave it unsaid. But it's as if you know what the other person wants and intends, when you've skimped along in two rooms together and stuck at it for over twenty years. I never think about him, really, any more than I would about my own hand – but it would be a nasty surprise if the hand were suddenly to became a foot, or go wandering off by itself . . . And then this! At first I thought: nonsense! Togo would *never* have done that. But then I said to myself: No one should be too sure, and hadn't we heard both on the radio and in speeches, and didn't it say on posters both in the metro and on the streets: NO ONE CAN BE CERTAIN! THE PERSON WHO IS CLOSEST TO YOU MAY BE A TRAITOR! I hadn't paid much attention to it before, I didn't think it concerned me. But what I went through in just one night I can't tell you. If my hair hadn't been grey before, after that night it was. It was so inconceivable to think that Togo, my Togo, was a traitor. But what do traitors look like? Don't they look like other people? It's only inside that they're different. Otherwise there would be no deception. And pretending to be like other people, that's obvious, it shows just how insidious they are. Yes, so I lay there and remade Togo for myself. And when I woke up in the morning, indeed, he was no longer a human being in my eyes. NO ONE CAN BE CERTAIN! THE PERSON WHO IS CLOSEST TO YOU MAY BE A TRAITOR! He was no longer human, he was worse than a wild beast. For a while I thought it was a bad dream – for there he stood, shaving just as he usually did – and I thought that if I could improve his ideas everything would be like normal again. But then I thought that you can't do that with traitors, for they don't improve, and just listening to someone like that can be dangerous enough. For he is rotten inside. So I telephoned the police as soon as I got to work, it was really the only thing I could do, if he was what he was. Of course I thought they'd arrest him right away, and when he came home in the evening as usual, I was waiting for the police to arrive at any moment. He noticed it, and then he said: "You've informed on me to the police. You shouldn't have done that. It was an experiment, and now you've ruined it all." But, tell me, how could I believe him just like that? How could I believe that he was human again? When I finally realized that it was true – yes, I wanted to throw my arms around him in delight, but can you imagine, he was angry. And *then he wanted a divorce.*'

'That was indeed quite remarkable,' was all I could say.

She swallowed repeatedly, so as not to embarrass herself by crying.

'You see, I want to hold on to him,' she continued. 'And I don't think it's fair that he wants a divorce, when I haven't done anything wrong.'

That was true, she was right. She shouldn't be punished for having acted like a good and trustworthy fellow soldier, she should be rewarded. She should be allowed to keep her Togo.

'He said he thought he couldn't trust me any more,' she went on, with many swallows. 'But of course he can trust me, if he's a human being. And it's also clear that no traitor can trust me, Kadidja Kappori!'

The image of that haggard woman's transfigured face arose in my memory with a forlorn hopelessness. What an immature and senseless demand, to want to have a person of one's own to trust, trust in a purely personal way, irrespective of what he or she does! I had to admit to myself that there was a lulling seduction in it. Perhaps the infant and the Stone Age savage live on not only in some of us but in us all, though in some more than others, and that is the important difference. And just as I felt it my duty to crush the pale woman's dream, so I considered the need to crush the same illusion in Kadidja Kappori's husband, even if it meant sacrificing one more night off.

'Come back and see me, both of you, during one of these times,' I said, writing down on a piece of paper the hours when I would be free. 'If he doesn't change course he'll be hearing from me.'

She took her leave with many expressions of thanks, and I escorted both her and the doctor out through the door. The doctor seemed to treat the whole matter as entertainment; he had sat all the time chuckling, and was still chuckling as he returned to his apartment. I was unable to take it that way. I could see the essential implications of the matter too clearly to be really interested in the ridiculous people who were involved.

I could not resist telling the story to Rissen during laboratory hours. Really it had nothing to do with our work, but it possessed a general significance none the less. I also strongly suspect that I was driven by a certain desire to show myself as being interesting and independent, the kind of man to whom others turned in their travails and who lightly and playfully helped them to put things right. The truth of the matter was that, harsh as my criticisms of Rissen were, and however deep my mistrust of him, I attached an equal importance to his estimation of me. Each time I caught myself trying to impress him I felt ashamed of myself and fended off my weakness. But a quarter of an hour later there it was again, and I did all I could to force some kind of esteem out of this strange man whom no one could respect. When I sensed that I had failed, I at least tried to irritate him, with the thought that a conscious plan lay behind my little tricks: if I could make him really annoyed I would at least know where I was with him, I told myself.

Among other things, there was mention of Kadidja Kappori's words: 'He was no longer human.'

'Human!' I said. 'Such a mystique people have built up around that word! As if there were something worthy of respect about being human! It's a biological concept, after all. Where it's anything else, it will be best to get rid of it as quickly as possible.'

Rissen merely looked at me with an expression that was hard to interpret.

'For example, this Kadidja Kappori,' I went on. 'In order to act correctly she had first to free herself of the inhibitions that lay in the superstitious notion that her husband was "human", in quotes – as from a biological point of view he could never in a thousand years be anything else. She was able to deal with that crisis in a single night, but how many people do that? A little slower on the uptake and she would have found herself among the traitors, without knowing how it had happened, all because of that superstition . . . I think we shall have to begin from the beginning and teach people to stop seeing the "human", with quotes, in the fellow soldier.'

'I don't think very many are victims of that sort of mystique,' said Rissen, slowly, as he stood with his eye to a burette he had just filled.

This was not a very remarkable statement, and nothing to raise any eyebrows, either. But he had a way of dropping his words in your ear, as though they concealed a special significance. This had the effect of always raising questions in my mind about what he had said, and his words, with his voice and intonation, came back and disturbed me.

In other respects that week turned out to be so full of exciting events that I forgot everything else on account of them. Indeed, they were even so important that they marked the beginning of Kallocain's victory march through the World State. But I shall save them for later, in order to finish the story of the Bahara–Kappori couple.

They came to see me just a week after Kadidja Kappori's first visit. Linda was once again busy with her banquet committee, but as I was now sure of the intentions of both of them and knew that I could at least keep Bahara in check, I didn't bother to call any witnesses. They both looked sullen and depressed, so it was clear that no reconciliation had yet taken place.

'Well, well,' I said, to help them along (it was best to take the whole thing with good humour), 'well, well, it looks as though your overtime pay was on the low side this time, Fellow Soldier Bahara. You know, a divorce could almost be called a permanent injury. Incidentally, that crutch – is it part of your job, or is it – hmm – an expression of your marital situation?'

He made no reply, just sat looking sullen. His wife nudged him:

'You should at least answer your chief, Togo, dear! Yes, imagine being married for twenty years and then filing for divorce because of this! It's really unfair, first you come and deceive me with an experiment and then get angry because I draw conclusions!'

'If you can put me in prison you can also manage without me if I walk free,' the husband replied bitterly.

'That's not the same at all!' she objected. 'If you'd been the person you tried to make me believe you were I would never have let you into the house! But since you aren't that person, but are still the one I've known for twenty years, I obviously want you to stay! And I've done nothing wrong, nothing to deserve you leaving me.'

'Answer me this, Fellow Soldier Bahara,' I said, in a less jocular tone this time. 'Do you really consider that your wife did something wrong when she denounced you?'

'I don't know if it was wrong, exactly . . .'

'What would you yourself do if someone came and told you he was a spy? . . . It won't take you too long to answer that, I hope. Shall I tell you what you should do? Go straight to the nearest mailbox, or use the nearest telephone and denounce him as soon as possible. That's right, isn't it? That's what you would do?'

'Yes, yes, of course – but it's not really the same.'

'I'm pleased to hear that's what you would do, as otherwise you would be committing a crime. It's also exactly what your wife has done. What do you mean, it's not really the same?'

This he found difficult to explain. There ensued a few hesitant attempts:

'That she really can believe anything at all about me . . . After twenty years! From one day to the next! And actually: just think if I really did come to her one day and tell her that I'd done something stupid and didn't for the life of me know what to do . . .'

'Then it would be too late to have regrets. And as for believing anything at all – don't you know that it's our duty to be suspicious? The State's welfare demands it. Twenty years is a long time, it's true, but one *can* make mistakes over twenty years. No, you have nothing to complain about.'

'No – but if she – I wouldn't . . .'

'Watch your tongue, dear Fellow Soldier, you might easily destroy my good opinion of your honour. Your wife denounced a spy. Was that right or wrong?'

'Yes – well– I suppose in the end it was right.'

'So: it was right. She denounced a spy, but the spy was not you. And now you want to divorce her because she did the right thing in relation to someone who was not you. Is that a rational thing to do?'

'But – it feels – so uncertain – when I look at her don't know what she thinks of me.'

'If I were you, I would beware of divorcing my wife on the grounds that she acted correctly. Quite apart from the fact that your profession does not attract women to you – nor your physical condition either, for that matter – so no decent woman would look at you twice when she got to know this story – and I dare say I would see to it that it got out – and then you would be landed with a stigma that everyone would talk about.'

'But I don't like this,' the man mumbled, more and more confused. 'I don't want it to be like this.'

'I must say, you surprise me,' I said, in a voice that grew ever colder. 'Will I have to conclude that you're an asocial type? You know, we shall really have to keep this affair in mind at the laboratory. It might not be so pleasant to have a label like that stuck to you.'

It worked. His confusion acquired a new tone of fright. Helplessly he transferred his fixed gaze from his wife and back to me again. After a short pause I resumed:

'But I'm sure you didn't mean any harm. You wanted to be sure that your wife had also dropped her suspicions. And she has, you can see that now. So there is no longer any reason for a divorce? Am I right?'

'Y-yes,' he agreed, relieved by my kindness, even though he

could not really follow my train of thought. 'Of course. There are no reasons – for divorce.'

The wife, who, on the other hand, grasped at once that the danger was now over and everything was as before, beamed with great relief. Her gratitude would have to be my sole compensation for the two nights off I had sacrificed. While Togo Bahara's sullen coolness disturbed me, it would probably wear off eventually. To help him along, I shouted after them:

'Later, you must come and report to me if your husband meant what he said, or if he really is an asocial type!'

Bahara knew that I was his chief. Kadidja Kappori's marriage was saved.

CHAPTER 7

That particular week our experiment had turned out to be unusually successful. No fewer than three of the group of ten were missing from the list of those who had been denounced, and fortunately the police had also been quick off the mark in making the arrests; so we had three independent and unsuspecting subjects at our disposal. Police Chief Karrek himself took part in the investigation. Tall and thin, he sat down on his chair, stretched his long legs straight before him, clasped his hands over his narrow torso, and waited with a mysterious fire in the slits of his eyes. The police chief was a remarkable person, the sort of man who seemed to be born to go far. His posture could be slack, even slacker than Rissen's, and yet he never looked unmilitary. While Rissen was carried along by his own impulses and seemed to drift rather than steer, Karrek's sunken repose was merely the lull before the leap, and in the hard, closed features, in the glitter behind his half-closed eyelids one could read that it would be the leap of a wild beast that never missed its prey. Not only did I feel respect for his physical strength, I also pinned my hopes to his power. Soon it would turn out that there my calculations had been correct.

The three remand prisoners were brought in one at a time and questioned. Two of them were of a sort we had not so far had to deal with, ordinary criminal types, who had quite simply been unable to resist the lure of the sums of money the spy was said to have promised. One of them, a woman, actually cheered up both us and the police chief with her intimate confessions about her husband's nature and habits. An intelligent woman, and witty, but not desirable as a fellow soldier, with the most compact individual selfishness.

The third, however, gave us something to think about.

Why he had not denounced his wife lay shrouded in mystery, clearly also to himself. On the one hand he showed none of the ecstatic gratitude for his wife's confession of the kind that the pale little woman we had previously questioned had shown, and on the other he had no interest in the promised sums of money, either. Even though he had not directly denied the possibility that his wife might be a spy, he was visibly uncertain that everything had happened the way she told it. All in all, one could perhaps say that a certain obtuseness had prevented him – an obtuseness he might perhaps have overcome a few days later, it was impossible to know. Had Karrek not already decided to let mercy take precedence over justice, that obtuseness would already have labelled him as treasonous. While an obtuse person of that kind was getting ready for action, a whole act of treachery might already have been performed, and the damage done; but not only that: his general tentativeness also bore witness to a very meagre devotion to the State. It came as no surprise, then, when among other things he let slip:

'All that is so much less important than *our* cause.'

I pricked up my ears, and I saw the police chief do the same.

'*Your* cause?' I asked. 'Who are *you*, then?'

He shook his head with a slightly foolish smile.

'Don't ask,' he said. 'We have no name, no organization. We just exist.'

'How can you exist, how can you call yourselves *we*, if you have neither name nor organization? How many of you are there?'

'Many, many. But I don't know how many. I have seen many, but don't know the names of most of them. Why would you need to know that? We know that they're *us*.'

As he was already showing signs of waking up, I looked questioningly first at Rissen, then at the police chief.

'By all means, continue,' Karrek murmured indistinctly. Rissen also made a positive sign. So I gave the man another injection.

'Well, go on: the names of those you know?'

In perfect cheerfulness and innocence, without the slightest hesitation, he reeled off five names. That was all, he said. He did not know any more. Karrek signalled to Rissen to write them down carefully, which he did.

'And what sort of insurrection is it that you want to carry out?'

In spite of the drug, he gave no answer. He turned and twisted under the question, and visibly exerted himself, but was unable to get anything out. For a moment I thought once again that perhaps under certain circumstances Kallocain might not take effect, and felt the cold sweat begin to trickle. But the question could also have been badly phrased, too complicated – though it was something they all must know, it seemed simple enough to me – so that the test subject could not have answered it even when awake.

'You want something, don't you?' I asked cautiously.

'Yes, yes of course, of course we want something . . .'

'And what is it?'

Once again silence. Then, with both hesitation and effort:

'We want to be – we want to be – something different –'

'Oh? And what do you want to be?'

Silence. A deep sigh.

'Some particular positions you want to take over?'

'No, no. Not that.'

'You want to be something different from fellow soldiers in the World State?'

'N-n-no – or rather, that is – no, not that –'

I was bewildered. Then Police Chief Karrek drew his legs towards him with a soundless movement, stretched forward over his own clasped hands, peered at the man and said in a low, penetrating voice:

'Where did you meet the others?'

'At the home of one of the ones I don't know.'

'Where? And when?'

'District RQ – two weeks ago last Wednesday . . .'

'How many were there?'

'Fifteen or twenty.'

'Then it won't be hard to find out who they were,' said Karrek, turning to Rissen and me. 'The concierge should know.'

And he continued the interrogation:

'You had permits, of course? Were they under false names?'

'Not under false names. At least, my permit was genuine.'

'All the easier, then. Well, go on. What was being discussed?'

But there even Karrek had to admit defeat. The interrogee's answer was confused and uncertain.

We had to leave the muddled fellow in peace, even more so as the injection was already beginning to wear off. He woke up with acute nausea. Psychologically, he did not seem to suffer too much, he was restless but not desperate, surprised rather than ashamed.

When the man had gone out through the doorway, the police chief drew himself up to the full extent of his elastic height, breathed deeply, as though he were sniffing the air, and said:

'We have some work to do here. The fellow knew nothing; that much is certain. His comrades will know more. We can make our way from one name to the next until we reach the innermost circles. Perhaps it's a real major conspiracy, who knows?'

He closed his eyes, and a look of satisfaction passed over his tensed features, smoothing them out. I guessed what he was thinking: this would carry his fame throughout the whole of the World State. It is possible that my guess was wrong. The police chief and I were very different by nature.

'Incidentally,' the police chief continued slowly, with a searching look at each of us in turn, 'incidentally, I'm going to be away for a short time. It's possible that you too will soon be summoned to another place. At any rate, get yourselves ready to travel. The summons may come while you are at home or at work. To be on the safe side, keep a packed suitcase at the laboratory so you don't need to waste time fetching it, a small suitcase with the most essential items, so you can stay away for a few days. And make sure the apparatus is working, so you can take it with you to show how your Kallocain works.'

'And my military duty?' asked Rissen.

'If anything comes up I'll make all the arrangements, of

course. If I can't, then nothing will come of it. I don't promise anything. And what are you going to do in the next few days?'

'More and more experiments.'

'Then is there anything to stop you following this thread? I mean the one we got from the last man you questioned. Instead of using the Voluntary Sacrifice Service you could unravel, inch by inch, that tangle of names of which he gave you one thread, write down exactly everything that transpires, and then wait. What do you say?'

Rissen thought it over.

'There's nothing about anything like that in the laboratory's rules and regulations.'

The police chief laughed an indescribably contemptuous laugh, delivered in a falsetto.

'We mustn't be bureaucratic,' he said. 'If an order comes in from the Head of Laboratory – that's Muili, isn't it – I don't think you need to stick to the rules and regulations too strictly. I shall go straight to Muili. Then all that needs to be done is to hand in all the names to police headquarters. The destiny of the World State may hang in the balance – and you ask about the rules and regulations!'

He left, and we looked at each other. I suspect that I looked both confident of victory and full of admiration. One could leave one's fate in the hands of a man like Karrek with an easy mind. He was made of pure will – there were no problems for him.

But Rissen raised his eyebrows with resignation.

'We're becoming a sub-department of the police,' he said. 'Farewell, science.'

This made me start. I loved my scientific work, and would sorely miss it if I lost it. But Rissen was just a pessimist, I assured myself. For my own part, all I could see ahead of me was the Staircase, and the first and only question was: did it lead upwards? As for the rest, time would tell.

Sure enough, an hour later an order arrived from the Head of Laboratory, telling us to rearrange our work along the lines the police chief had indicated. Police headquarters had already been informed, and all we had to do was telephone with the names of those we wanted to be arrested – then the individuals in question would be available to us within twenty-four hours.

The first one we got was a young man not long out of youth camp, with an amusing blend of insecurity and arrogant aggression against the social life to which he did not yet feel quite adjusted. Under the influence of Kallocain his self-assurance had room to expand in a way that struck us adult men as comical, and he began to entertain us with far-reaching and extremely vague plans for the future. At the same time he admitted that he usually felt deeply burdened by the people around him. They meant him harm, he said. It was true that I myself had suggested that we should let our test subjects talk about themselves as much as possible, as the previous case had been so hard to question. But here there was slightly too much youthful psychology to imagine that Karrek got much joy from it, so in the end I proceeded to interrogate the man, and asked him if he knew our previous subject.

'Yes, we're work colleagues.'

'Have you ever met him outside work?'

'Yes. He invited me to a meeting . . .'

'In District RQ? Two weeks ago last Wednesday?'

The young man began to laugh, and at the same time appeared to be very interested.

'Yes. An odd sort of meeting. But I liked them. In a way, I liked them . . .'

'Can you tell us what you remember?'

'Of course. It was so peculiar, though. When I got in I didn't know any of the people there. Well, that wasn't so strange, really. If you give up your night off for social life, it's usually in order to discuss something, something that affects your work or something else, plans for a party or a letter to the authorities or that sort of thing, and then obviously you won't know all the guests. But it was nothing like that! They didn't discuss anything at all. They sat and chatted about all kinds of stuff, or else they were silent. The fact that they were silent so much made me really scared. And by the way, how they greeted one another! They took each other by the hand. It isn't wise. It must be unhygienic, and also so intimate that you'd be ashamed

to do it. Touching one another's bodies like that, deliberately!
They said it was an ancient greeting that they'd revived, but
you didn't have to do it if you didn't want to, there was no
compulsion to do anything. But at first I was afraid of them.
There's nothing worse than sitting in silence. You have a feeling that people are looking through you. As though you were
naked or worse than naked. Spiritually naked. Especially when
there are older people there, as they may have had time to learn
to see through others, and so when they talk they have learned
how to talk on the surface and be on their guard under the surface. There have already been times when I've been able to do
that, talk on the surface and be on my guard under the surface,
and then one felt relieved afterwards, as though a danger had
been avoided. But I couldn't do it there. None of them would
have taken the bait. When they talked, they talked softly, and
they looked as though they weren't thinking of anything else.
In general, I think it's better to talk loudly so as to catch other
people's attention, to talk loudly and have your mind elsewhere. But they were so peculiar. In the end I thought it was
nice, and began to like them. It was calm, in a way.'

    This was not very enlightening. The young fellow was, after
all, a novice in the movement, and not yet initiated into its
secrets. To make sure, I also asked him:

    'Did you see if the group had a leader? Were there any dis-
tinctions of rank?'

    'No – not that I saw. No one said anything about that,
either.'

    'And what did you actually do? Did they talk about any-
thing they had done or were going to do?'

    'Not as far as I know. Though I had to leave early, of course,
I and a few others who hadn't been there before either, I think.
I don't know what they did after that. But when we left, there
was someone who said: "When we meet in the world outside
we'll recognize one another." I can't explain it, but it was really
quite impressive, and I actually thought I would recognize
them – not exactly the people I met there, but anyone who
belonged, who was one of *them*. There was something special
about them, I can't describe it. When I came into this room I

was absolutely certain that *you* didn't belong there (he nodded at me). But *you'* (he gave Rissen a hazy look), 'you I'm not so sure about. Maybe you belong here and maybe you don't. All I know is that I felt calmer with them than with others. I didn't have such a clear sense that they meant me harm.'

I gave Rissen a sharp glance. He looked so dumbfounded that I thought he was probably innocent, if by innocent one meant that he had never taken part in secret meetings like the one the young man described. Yet there was something in the insinuation. In Rissen, too, there were the same asocial tendencies, an affinity with blind moles.

The young man woke with a sense of remorse that was not proportionate to the perfectly harmless things he had revealed. As far as I could tell, his anguish was caused not by the story about the meeting, but by the purely personal confessions we had brought to a halt with our yawns.

'I think I'll have to retract a lot of what I said,' he mumbled, as he stood swaying on the floor. 'What I said about being unsure of others, that wasn't really true. I just wonder what they think of me. I'm not implying that they necessarily mean me harm. And everything I said about what I wanted to be and do, that was just pure fantasy, not one drop of truth. I was also exaggerating when I said that I felt more comfortable with those peculiar folk than with ordinary people. Of course I feel more comfortable with ordinary people, when I think about it . . .'

'We are convinced of that too,' said Rissen, kindly. 'In future you should probably stick to the others, the ordinary ones. We have a strong suspicion that the meetings, one of which you so inadvertently attended, are treasonable. It's clear that you have not yet really been infected, but watch out! Before you know where you are, they'll have trapped you in their nets.'

The young man looked frightened as he retreated through the doorway.

I do not know what terrible plans we really expected to uncover from the meeting that resumed after the young man and the others like him had been sent home from the gathering. At any rate, some of the remand prisoners must have been there when the plans were hatched. We subjected the four who still remained to thorough and systematic questioning; we made a careful record of their stories, but it was a long time before we obtained anything like a clear picture of the secret society. On many occasions we could only look at one another and shake our heads. Was it a gathering of the mentally ill that we had on our hands? I had seldom heard tell of anything more fantastical.

First of all, we were in pursuit of the organization itself, the names of the superiors, the structure. But time after time we were told that there were no leaders, there was no organization. Now in secret conspiracies it is often the case that members of lower rank do not have access to secrets of a more central nature; all they know are the names of two or three other members who are as insignificant as themselves. We deduced that it was members like this we had got hold of. Nevertheless, it was likely that from some of those we had already caught we would reach new levels where people knew more. It was simply a matter of persevering.

Our most immediate question was what had happened after the novices left the building. One woman gave us a surprising description.

'They take out a knife,' she said. 'One of us hands it to another and lies down on a bed and pretends to be asleep.'

'Well, and then what?'

'That's all. If someone else wants to join in, and there's room for it, he can also pretend to be sleeping. You can sit down and lean your head on the edge of the bed. Or the table or whatever.'

I am afraid that I let out a stifled laugh. The scene that one imagined was too priceless. Someone sat there earnestly holding a large table knife (of course it was a table knife, that was the easiest to obtain, one simply forgot to leave it on one's dinner plate), in the midst of an equally earnest crowd. One man had stretched himself out on the bed with his hands on his stomach, making convulsive efforts to go to sleep, even perhaps trying to snore. One after the other, they pulled out a pillow and placed it nearby, leaned their heads in a more or less uncomfortable position, and added their little snore to the pile. Someone slid down into a sitting position, along the edge of the bed, stretched his legs, leaned the back of his head against the wooden frame, yawned ... Otherwise, dead silence.

Not even Rissen could suppress a slight smile.

'And what does it all mean?' he asked.

'It has a symbolic meaning. Through the knife he has surrendered to the other's power, and yet nothing happens to him.'

(Nothing happens to him! When the room is full of people all around, snoring but in reality wide awake and ready to open one eye at any moment! Nothing happens to him, when his guests – quite lawfully registered with the janitor – sit clutching a knife with which they sought in vain to cut the boiled beef, and listen to how naturally he is snoring ...)

'And what purpose does it serve, all that?'

'We want to summon forth a new spirit,' the woman answered, with perfect seriousness.

Rissen scratched his chin reflectively. At State history lectures I had heard, and so had Rissen, probably, that prehistoric savages used to utter certain adjurations and perform certain so-called magic rituals in order to summon imaginary beings they called spirits. And such things still happened in our day?

From the same woman, we managed to elicit some information about a complete fool who seemed to play a certain role as the hero within their circle. My goodness, it does not take much to be considered a hero among some people.

'Don't you know about Reor?' she asked. 'No, he's not alive now, he lived about fifty years ago, in one of the mill cities, some say, but others say in one of the textile cities. Imagine not having heard of Reor. I'd like to give lectures about Reor some time. Though it's true that only the initiated can understand. If you want to talk about Reor, you must turn to the initiated. He travelled around here and there, for in those days the situation with permits was different, and some people took him in out of fear, as they thought he worked for the police and others chased him away. But of course not all of those who took him in – nor indeed anyone else – noticed what he was really like. Some thought he was simply peculiar, but others felt they could be secure and calm with him, like a little child with its mother. Some forgot him, but others never forgot him, and they told others about him as best they could. But only the initiated understand it. He never locked his door. He never cared about witnesses or evidence of something he said or did. He never even protected himself from thieves and murderers, so in the end he was murdered by a robber who thought he had a loaf of bread in his knapsack. Those were times of hunger. But he didn't have any bread, he had already eaten it all together with some other people he had met along the way ... But the other man thought he had saved it. So he killed him.'

'And yet you think he was a great man?' I asked.

'He was a great man. Reor was a great man. He was one of us. There are still people living who saw him.'

Rissen gave me a meaningful look and shook his head.

'The most expensive logic I have heard in all my life,' I said. 'Let us be like him, because he was murdered! I don't understand any of it.'

'You spoke of initiation,' Rissen said to the woman, without paying attention to me. 'How do people become initiated?'

'I don't know. You just do. All of a sudden, and then you are. The others notice it, the ones who are also initiated.'

'So anyone can come along and say he's initiated? There must be some ritual, some ceremony – some secrets that are shared?'

'No, nothing like that. It's something you notice, I tell you. You see, it's something you either are or you aren't – some people never are.'

'How would you notice it?'

'Well, you notice it in everything – in the knife and the sleep, and when it dawns on you with holy clarity – and many other things –'

We were no wiser than before.

Whether only the woman was crazy or whether all those people shared her craziness, it was hard to tell. While it was clear that the magic rituals with the knife and the pretend sleeping really had taken place, for we had the others' confirmation of those, it remained unclear if they took place regularly or were an occasional event. Nor could we find traces of the

Reor myth in all the subjects, though it did remain in some of them. What, then, was the common characteristic that held this circle together, apart from the fact that they all, every one of them, seemed strange?

Another person, also a woman, had a few names to give us. We therefore considered it appropriate to press her particularly hard on the subject of the organization. Her answer was just as confusing as those of the others.

'Organization?' she said. 'We seek no organization. What is organic doesn't need to be organized. You build from outside, we are built from inside. You build with yourselves like stones and fall apart from outside, and in. We are built from inside, like trees, and between us grow bridges that are not made of dead matter and dead coercion. From us the living emerges. In you the lifeless enters.'

All this struck me as a meaningless play on words, and yet it made an impression on me. Perhaps it was the intensity in her deep voice that made me tremble. It is not impossible that it reminded me of Linda, who also has a deep and intense voice, especially at times when she doesn't seem so tired. I couldn't help imagining how it would have been if instead of the strange woman, it was Linda sitting there, handing me her innermost being in such pleading and penetrating tones. At any rate I kept it in my memory for a long time afterwards, even repeated the individual words to myself, because I thought they sounded beautiful in all their meaninglessness. Much, much later I began to glimpse a meaning in them. At any rate this woman's words shocked me even then, so that I had my first sense of what they meant by 'we', how they recognized one another and how they were able to have a circle of initiates without an organization, without outward identifying marks and clearly even without any generally embraced teachings or doctrines.

When she had been released and allowed to go, I said to Rissen:

'Something has occurred to me. Perhaps we misunderstood that bit about a "spirit". It can also mean an inner shape, an attitude to life. Or do you think that's too subtle an interpretation to be applied to such a group of fools?'

When he looked at me I grew afraid. I could see by his bearing that he understood me completely, but there was also something else. I realized that he too had been affected by the woman's warm and intense presence. I realized that he was even more susceptible than I was. And I realized that his very gaze, his very silence, were drawing me in a direction where my love of duty and sense of honour forbade me to go. In some way he was caught in the net of those fools, and even I had for a moment felt the sweet and overwhelming attraction.

Had not the first young man today said of Rissen that he might well belong there – to the fools, to the secret sect? Had I myself not always had a feeling that in Rissen there was a threat and a danger? From now on I knew that deep down we were enemies.

We had only one of the remand prisoners left, an ageing man of intelligent appearance, and I was at once afraid of him – no one could know if he might have the same suggestive power as the woman just then – and expected great things of him. He, if anyone, ought to know something about the innermost circles, and with a bit of good luck we might find such damning evidence that the whole sect of fools would be condemned and dispatched, to the relief and salvation of myself and many others. But when he had been brought in and we had more or less managed to get him seated in the chair, the internal phone rang, and both Rissen and I were summoned to see Muili, the head of the laboratory.

CHAPTER 8

Muili's office was not in our laboratory building, but it wasn't necessary to go up to the surface in order to get there: a corridor three floors below led straight across to the building where the laboratory's clerical staff worked, and after you had shown your identity card and a secretary had made sure on the telephone that you were expected, you could proceed. Twenty-five minutes later we stood face to face with Muili, a very thin, steely-grey-haired man of sickly appearance. He hardly looked at us. His voice was soft, as though he could scarcely manage to speak, and yet its every tone was that of a command. This man was not used to listening to anyone else except in answers to direct questions.

'Fellow Soldiers Edo Rissen and Leo Kall,' he said, 'you have been called to another place. You are to discontinue the work you are currently doing. Within the hour a police escort will take you to the point of departure. All arrangements regarding your temporary leave from military and police duty have been made. Understood?'

'Yes, my chief,' Rissen and I replied together.

In silence we returned to the laboratory to set things in order, shower and put on our leisure uniforms. We each had a small suitcase for the journey, and a container for the Kallocain apparatus that Karrek had ordered us to bring. At the appointed time two taciturn police officers arrived, and took us by metro to our destination.

My admiration for Karrek rose further. Indeed, quick march! Barely a day had passed since he left, and already he had got what he wanted. The man was a powerhouse, and not only in Chemistry City No. 4, it seemed.

When we emerged from the metro our objective turned out to be an aircraft hangar. A shiver of joy in adventure passed through my body. How far were we going? To the capital? I, who had never been outside Chemistry City No. 4, was gripped by the wildest excitement.

Together with a group of other passengers we entered the well-lit aeroplane, the police officers locked and sealed the door, and from the hum of the engines we realized that we were airborne. I took the latest issue of *Chemical Journal* from my suitcase, and Rissen did likewise, but I noticed that like me he often leaned back and let his thoughts fly around other matters besides the articles and announcements in the journal. As for myself, I tried to restrain my curiosity as soon as it reared its head. In films I had of course seen yellow fields, green meadows, forests, grazing sheep and cows, even aerial photographs, so strictly speaking I had nothing to be curious about, and yet I had to fight a ridiculous and childish wish that the plane had just one little peephole through which one could secretly look – not because I was intent on espionage, but out of sheer childish curiosity. At the same time I knew that this was a dangerous tendency. I would certainly never have got so far in science if a certain curiosity had not driven me into the mysteries of matter – on the other hand, it was a driving force for good or ill, and could lure one into danger and criminal behaviour. I wondered if Rissen had the same inclinations and desires to struggle with – if he ever did, that was! With his lack of discipline, he was not the kind of man who struggled. I had the impression that he sat there, quite without struggle or shame, wishing that the plane were made entirely of glass ... A most accurate impression, I thought; that was what the man was like. If only I could use Kallocain for my own private amusement ...

I had nodded off when I felt a gentle nudge at my elbow. The flight attendant stood there, serving the evening meal – that, too, was taken care of. I looked at my wrist watch: we had already been flying for five hours and clearly still had some way to go, as the serving of the meal indicated. My calculation was correct: we still had three hours to go. With a knowledge not only of the time needed for the journey but also of the speed of the plane one could have easily worked out the distance between Chemistry City No. 4 and our destination, whatever it might be, but fortunately the speed of the plane was kept strictly secret, so that no spies could draw geographical conclusions. All one could assume was that the speed was very great, and the distance likewise. As for the direction, we could of course draw no conclusions about that: the fact that the air was cool, even cold, by Chemistry City standards, simply meant that we were travelling at some height.

When finally we landed and the engines died, the door was unlocked by a small group of police, who then split up and attended to the various passengers. (Presumably everyone there was on important business, announced and expected, or perhaps summoned like us.) Rissen and I were taken down to the police and military metro, where our carriage hurtled at incredible speed to a station called Police Palace. We assumed that we were in the capital. Through an underground portal we were taken to an antechamber, where we were bodysearched and our luggage was examined, and then up to some simple but perfectly serviceable cabin-like rooms, where we were to sleep.

CHAPTER 9

At breakfast time next morning we were shown up to one of the refectories. We were clearly not the only overnight guests at the Police Palace – in the great hall about seventy other fellow soldiers of both sexes and all adult ages were already crowding around the self-service tables. Someone waved to us from his seat. It was Karrek, who had settled down with his cornmeal porridge among a group of strangers. No matter how superior to us he was in rank, we felt really glad to see his familiar face, and he did not look as if he had any objection to our company, either.

'I've applied for an audience with the police president for all three of us,' he said, 'and I have reason to believe that it won't take long. You should fetch the equipment as soon as possible.'

I naturally hurried to finish my breakfast and rushed off to fetch the Kallocain apparatus. My haste subsequently proved to be somewhat unnecessary. After all three of us had been escorted down to the police president's waiting room, we had to wait more than an hour before the door to the inner chamber was opened. Moreover, three people sat waiting before us, so I guessed that we would be there for some time.

But as it turned out, we were first in line. An agile little official opened the door, went over to Karrek and whispered to him. Karrek pointed to us, and all three of us were led into another waiting room, where we were body-searched again. In general the security here was much more thorough than back home in our chemistry city, for the obvious reason that the lives that had to be protected here were much more rare and valuable than in any other part of the World State. Even out in the waiting room, and much more so here in the antechamber and in the police president's office itself, there were guards with raised pistols. But at last we stood before the powerful man.

A broad-shouldered figure turned round in his chair and raised his bushy eyebrows in greeting. It was clear that he was rather pleased to see Karrek. I recognized Police Minister Tuareg at once from the *Fellow Soldier's Portrait Album*, his small, black bear-like eyes, his strong-willed lower jaw, his fleshy mouth and yet the impression he made on me was far more overwhelming than I had ever expected it to be. Perhaps, too, it was the sense of standing before concentrated Power that made me tremble. Tuareg was the brain behind those millions of eyes and ears that saw and heard the fellow soldiers' most intimate deeds and conversations day and night, he was the will behind those millions of arms that constantly or for certain parts of the day protected the State's internal security – including my own arms, in so far as my evenings were devoted to police duty. And yet I quaked, as though it were not my own supreme will I stood face to face with – as though instead I were one of the criminals he hunted. And yet I had done nothing wrong! Where did that ill-fated split in my being originate? The answer lay close at hand: it was all the result of a hypnotic delusion that might be expressed in the words: 'No fellow soldier over forty can have a clear conscience.' And the man who had spoken those words was Rissen.

'So-o, here we have our new associates,' said the police minister to Karrek. 'Would you be ready to perform some small sample experiments in two hours' time? On the third floor there is a room that has been set up as a laboratory – a primitive one, perhaps, but I think you will find it contains what you need. If anything is lacking, all you have to do is tell the staff. And we will put test subjects at your disposal.'

We declared ourselves ready and satisfied. The audience was over, and we were led out by a different way, and up to the temporary laboratory Tuareg had mentioned. The furniture and equipment were perfectly adequate, as long as there was no intention of producing Kallocain in large quantities.

Karrek had followed us up. He sat down at the corner of a

table in a posture so excessively casual that in anyone else it would have appeared slack and offensive.

'Well, Fellow Soldiers,' he said, after we had examined the room's potential for our work, 'what has emerged about that secret meeting back in Chemistry City No. 4?'

Rissen was my chief, and so had the right and duty to answer first. This he did, though only after a long silence.

'As far as I am concerned,' he said, 'I can't see that anything explicitly criminal has emerged. They all seem slightly deranged, but criminal – no.

'So far, at least,' he continued after another pause, 'we haven't come across anyone who is concealing an unlawful act, or at least an act that has preoccupied their thoughts sufficiently for them to reveal it under the influence of Kallocain. I exclude that man who omitted to denounce his wife for treason, for you will be aware, my chief, that we agreed to let mercy come before justice, since it's important to sustain recruitment to the Voluntary Sacrifice Service. As for the rest of these people, while I would call them a sect of fools, they are not a political association. Perhaps they can't even be called a sect. They have no organization, no leaders, as far as we can ascertain, no membership lists, not even a name, and so they don't really come under the law against associations beyond the State's control.'

'You really are a stickler for form, Fellow Soldier Rissen,' said Karrek, narrowing his eyes ironically. 'You speak of "rules and regulations" and "coming under the law", as if printer's ink were an insuperable obstacle. You don't really mean it, do you?'

'Laws and regulations are there for our protection . . .' Rissen objected, dourly.

'For *whose* protection, did you say?' Karrek parried. 'Not the State's, at least. The State has more use for clear heads that can despise printer's ink when necessary.'

Rissen was reluctantly silent, but then began again:

'Anyway, they don't seem to present a threat to the State. We can quietly release the ones who have already been arrested and then leave the whole bunch of them to their fate. The police will have their hands full with murderers, thieves, perjurers . . .'

My moment had arrived, I felt it. I had to make my first serious attack on Rissen.

'My chief, Karrek,' I said slowly and with strong emphasis. 'Permit me to raise objections, even though I am a subordinate. That strange society strikes me as being anything but innocent.'

'I'm interested in your opinion too,' said Karrek. 'So you think it's just an ordinary conspiracy?'

'I shall leave aside the paragraphs of the law for the moment,' I said. 'What I mean is that all those people, individually and as a group, present a danger to the State. First of all I would merely ask: do you think our World State stands in need of a totally new approach, a completely altered attitude to life? Yes, don't misunderstand me, I know that people both here and there might need to be awoken to a greater sense of responsibility and to greater efforts – but a new attitude to life, different from what we have known so far? Is that not an insult to the World State and the World State's fellow soldiers? And yet that was the implication of what one of the remand prisoners said: "We want to summon forth a new spirit." At first we understood the expression in a more specific sense, as a manifestation of superstition – but this is even worse.'

'I think you interpret it too harshly,' said Karrek. 'My experience has taught me that the more abstract something is the less dangerous are its effects. General turns of speech may be used any way one wants to twist them, now in one direction, a moment later in another that's the complete opposite.'

'But an ethos isn't something abstract,' I said heatedly. 'On the contrary, I would say that it's the only thing that is definitely not abstract. And the ethos of those fools is hostile to the State. One can see it most clearly in their own myths about a person called Reor, who seems to have been slightly ahead of the rest in mental deficiency, and has therefore become their special hero. Leniency towards criminals, carelessness with one's own security (one is oneself a valuable and sophisticated instrument, that shouldn't be forgotten!), personal ties that are stronger than one's bond to the State – that is where they want to lead us! At first glance their rituals look like pure buffoonery. On closer consideration they become overwhelmingly obnoxious. They are images of an exaggerated trust between people, or at least between certain people. That alone I consider to be treasonable. The ones who are too credulous will come to the same end as their hero Reor – sooner or later they will be robbed and murdered. *And was it not on this very foundation that the State was built?* If there were reason for trust between people, no State would have arisen. The sacred and necessary foundation of the State's existence is our mutual well-founded mistrust of each other. Those who cast suspicion on that foundation cast suspicion on the State.'

'Pah!' said Rissen, with a certain vehemence, 'you forget that it had to arise in any case, as an economic and cultural centre . . .'

'No, I don't,' I said. 'And please don't imagine that I'm arguing from some sort of civilian superstition that the State should exist for our sake instead of us for the sake of the State, as is actually the case. All I mean is that the kernel of the individual cells' relation to the State organism lies in the hunger for security. If one day we should notice – I don't say that we have done, but *if* – that our pea soup got thinner, our soap barely usable, our apartments decrepit, without anyone being concerned about the matter – would we grumble? No. We know that luxury is of no value in itself, that our sacrifices serve a higher purpose. And if we discover barbed-wire barricades across our roads, do we not put up with all restrictions on our freedom of movement without complaint? Yes. We know that all this is happening for the sake of the State, in order to deter wreckers. And if one day we should find that all leisure activities must be restricted for essential military exercises, that the countless branches of skill and knowledge that were previously part of our upbringing must now be set aside for an unavoidable emphasis on the special training of each and every one of us as workers in the service of absolutely essential industry – have we reason to complain then? No, no, and no. We realize and approve that the State is everything, the individual nothing. We realize and bow before the fact that most of so-called "culture" – I except the technical sciences – remains a luxury for epochs when no danger threatens (epochs that perhaps will never come again). What remains is naked survival, and the ever more developed military and police apparatus. That is the kernel of the State's life. All else is a façade.'

Rissen, dark and reflective, said nothing. He probably had trouble in finding any objections to my none-too-original speech, but I was certain – and gratified – that his civilian soul was experiencing cold shivers of irritation.

Karrek had jumped to his feet and started to pace back and forth. I had the impression that he was not listening too carefully to my arguments, and that pained me. When I had finished, he said with slight impatience:

'Yes, yes, that's all very fine. The fact is, however, that as far as I know we have never yet waged any struggle against "spirits". We have allowed them to haunt the unreal spheres where they belong. When people let their tongues run away with them at the dinner table or play truant from an official banquet, that is at least something one can take hold of, but "spirits" – no thank you . . .'

'Previously we've never had the means of doing it,' I objected. 'Kallocain gives us the possibility of controlling what goes on in people's minds.'

Not even now did he seem to listen to my argument with more than half an ear.

'Anyone can be judged and found guilty on that basis,' he said in a slightly peevish tone.

Suddenly he stopped and was motionless, struck, it appeared, by the implication of his own words.

'Anyone can be judged and found guilty on that basis,' he repeated, but this time with infinite slowness and softness and stillness. 'Anyway, perhaps you are not so wrong, when all things are considered – when all things – are considered . . .'

'But my chief, if you yourself say,' Rissen cried in horror, 'that anyone –'

Karrek did not hear him. He had resumed his pacing with long strides; his peculiar Mongolian head, with its half-closed eyes, stretched forwards.

I wanted to be of service to him, so I told him, though with a certain feeling of shame, about the reprimand I had got from the Seventh Bureau of the Ministry of Propaganda. That finally caught his attention.

'The Seventh Bureau of the Ministry of Propaganda, you say?' he said, thoughtfully. 'That's interesting. That's very interesting.'

A long while passed, during which the faint creaking of his soles was the only sound that was heard, apart from the distant alternating rumble of the metro and the murmur of voices and other noise from the neighbouring rooms. In the end he supported himself against the wall with his hand, closed his eyes and said slowly, as though he were weighing each word:

'Let me be completely frank. It is in our power to steamroller such a law on mental criminality through, if we have enough connections in the Seventh Bureau.'

Just then I do not think I had room in me for anything but servility, but I too was possibly infected by a gust from Karrek's dreams of grandeur, from plans and visions with which I myself was unfamiliar. At any rate, I caught my breath when he continued:

'I will send one of you, preferably one who speaks convincingly and well, to the Seventh Bureau. For certain reasons, I cannot go myself . . . Now then, Fellow Soldier Kall, can you phrase your words well? But I had better ask your superior. Can he?'

Only after a moment's hesitation did Rissen answer, almost unwillingly:

'He can, and eminently so.'

It was the first time I had noticed an open approach to antipathy on Rissen's part.

'Then let me talk to you alone, Fellow Soldier Kall.'

We withdrew to my cabin. Quite unembarrassed, Karrek stuffed a pillow against the police ear, and when I looked somewhat surprised, he said, laughing:

'Well, I am the chief of police, and in the unlikely event that the matter should be detected, I shall know where I am with Tuareg . . .'

I could not help admiring him for his very insolence, but it made me somewhat uneasy that he constantly climbed and chased along lines that were personal and not based on principle.

'Well, anyway,' he said. 'You'll have to think of something to talk about with Lavris at the Seventh Bureau. I would suggest that you take up the subject of that reprimand and link it to your discovery in some way. And then, in passing – I repeat, in passing, as legislation is not in itself one of the Seventh Bureau's tasks – you will mention how important it would become with our new law – this discovery, yours and mine . . . I must explain it to you: Lavris has influence with Law Minister Ta Cho . . .'

'But would it not be more practical to go straight to Law Minister Ta Cho?'

'No, it would be extremely impractical. Even if you had a definite errand, a specific and genuine errand, along with this law proposal, it would be weeks before you were admitted to see him, and we can't do without you in Chemistry City No. 4 for that long. If on the other hand all you had was the law proposal, it is highly improbable that you would be admitted at all; who are you, they would ask, to be making law proposals? The individual obeys the laws, but he doesn't make them. However, if Lavris takes a hand in the matter . . . But the main thing is to get her interested. Do you think you can do that?'

'I can't do any worse than fail,' I said. 'It's not as though I were exposing myself to danger.'

Inwardly I was convinced that I would succeed; it was the kind of task where I could employ the best of my skills. Karrek must also have deduced this when he probed me with his narrow gaze.

'Off you go, then,' he said. 'Your permit will be here tomorrow, and I will provide you with recommendations. Now you have permission to go back to your work.'

CHAPTER 10

We had to wait for Tuareg. When you are used to each and every minute of the day and night having an unshakable purpose, an empty space of this kind becomes extremely trying; but all things, even the worst, eventually pass, and at last the police minister arrived, so that we could demonstrate the uses to which Kallocain could be put. I had not really thought I would need to make such a determined effort not to let my hand tremble when an unshaven criminal's sleeve was rolled up in front of me, but Tuareg's little bear-eyes drilled into the back of my head so sharply that it almost felt like having an injection. However, everything went according to plan. Amid a stream of crude profanities that made the police minister's fleshy mouth twitch and thus lightened the mood somewhat, the subject made a full confession to the burglary with which he was charged but for which he had so far escaped punishment due to a lack of evidence. He also admitted to a large number of other crimes he had committed alone or with others, producing all the names and particulars without blinking. Tuareg's nostrils flared with relish.

We continued with other subjects. Rissen and I took turns at giving the injections, the police minister's personal secretary recorded the proceedings, and to test us further they had included a few innocent fellow soldiers along with the rest. Innocent of breaking the law, that is; in another sense the word proved to be more inapposite than one could possibly imagine, much to the police minister's obvious delight. After we had managed to get through six subjects in a remarkably short time, Tuareg stood up and declared that he was fully convinced.

Kallocain would replace all other methods of interrogation throughout the whole of the World State as soon as was possible, he said. He proposed to keep us in the capital for a few more days so that we could instruct some experts in injection work; in addition, when we got home again our task would be to train injectors from every region, and also, of course, Kallocain manufacturers from the chemistry cities, on a large scale. He left us with every sign of being in a good mood, and shortly afterwards we received some twenty individuals to whom we were to give training. The test subjects stood waiting in a long queue outside the door, all of them criminals brought directly from the remand centre.

The very next day I was summoned to see Karrek and received orders to leave all the work to Rissen, at least for now. He handed me a rather formidable bundle of papers, which consisted of permits, recommendations and identity documents of various kinds.

I think I have forgotten to say that the request for new propaganda for the Voluntary Sacrifice Service, which I had drafted and presented to the various institutes in Chemistry City No. 4, was fully signed and approved within a few days and I had taken all these signatures with me in order to deliver them in person to the Ministry of Propaganda. To be on the safe side I asked Karrek for advice on where to apply, and he gave me many good directions. My excellent recommendations would surely also be useful at the Third Bureau, under which propaganda of this kind was filed. So before long I was aboard the metro, and got out at the Ministry of Propaganda's imposing underground entrance.

That very morning I had felt an indisposition coming on, and the police ministry's staff doctor had been pumping me with all sorts of medicaments, so that I was now in a somewhat abnormal condition. This was probably why I had become so inexplicably agitated when requesting my interview with Lavris, the Head of the Seventh Bureau. After all, it was really Karrek's business I was on rather than my own, as he had seemed particularly keen on this law being passed for reasons that were obscure to me. But in my exalted condition I had a sense that I was not acting on Karrek's behalf, or even my own, but that my action was a link in the whole of the vast development of the State, perhaps one of the final links before completion was achieved. I, an insignificant cell in the great State organism, a cell poisoned, if only temporarily, by many and various drops and powders, was launching a work of purification that would free the State's body from all the sick poison the thought criminals had implanted there. When at last – after many formalities, body searches, periods of waiting – I rose to be admitted to Lavris's reception room, it was as though I were going to take my own purifying bath from which I would return calm and free from all the asocial dregs I did not want to acknowledge or recognize and which were not mine but lurked so insidiously in the dark corners of my being and which I could sum up under a single name: Rissen.

There was nothing in Lavris's office to distinguish the room from a thousand other offices, except for the guards with raised pistols who were posted here as they were at the police minister's office, indicating that those who worked within were rare and valuable instruments of the State. Yet I felt short of breath, and my temples throbbed. The tall, thin-necked woman at the desk, the skin over her mouth and cheeks tensed in a perpetual ironic smile, was Kalipso Lavris.

Even though her age was indeterminate and her posture stiff as an antique effigy, in my feverish state of mind I would probably have seen her as only half human. Not even a large pimple that had erupted on the left side of her nose and was clearly about to attain full ripeness could draw her down to earth in my eyes. Did she not function as the World State's highest ethical authority, or at least as the leading light in the World State's highest ethical authority, which was the Ministry of Propaganda's Seventh Bureau? In her face one could read no personal emotions as one could in Tuareg's, her immobility contained no hidden leaps as in Karrek's; to me she seemed to be crystal-cut logic itself, washed free of all the quirks of individuality. It was the fantasy of a fever dream, but for all its excess voltage it caught Lavris's image rather well, I suspect.

I had already known in advance that any suggestion for a

change in the law should not be made openly, as in official terms the Seventh Bureau had nothing to do with such a matter. The guards with their raised pistols were an even clearer reminder of this, though it did not trouble me. My errand was essential if the State, if I myself, were not to perish.

I do not really know how I broached the subject of the earlier reprimand. While they retrieved my secret police card I had to wait in a small waiting room for nearly two hours, I think. One must learn this, I thought, one must learn to wait. And I did. Yet it must be admitted that it all went rather quickly, when one considers the vast expanses such a card system of all the World State's fellow soldiers must fill. Although I had never seen it, I could very well imagine it would take at least an hour to walk through the enormous halls to where my card was (on the other hand, it must all be so precisely systematized that one did not need to spend a long time looking when one was actually there) and then the same journey back again. If it were also taken into account that the card system was housed not by the Ministry of Propaganda but by the police, one could be perfectly content with a two-hour wait.

When I was readmitted, Lavris sat studying my card – 'card' is actually a misnomer, for it looked more like a small, bound book – and beside it a thin packet of documents, which presumably contained preparatory notes and reports on the subject of my reprimand. It was of course easy to understand if she had forgotten all the details of the case, so busy must the Seventh Bureau be with the most important denunciations and issues from every part of the World State.

'Yes,' said Lavris, in her toneless and yet high voice, 'we have your case here. On your police card it says that you have already asked to be allowed to make your apology on the radio, though you have not yet had occasion to do so. What is it you really want?'

'I have had regard for the words: *unmasking of the former ones* – the disunited – *is a praiseworthy action in the State's best interests*,' I said. 'I have even made a discovery that makes it possible to unmask them more thoroughly and more systematically than before.'

And I told her about Kallocain as intriguingly as I could.

'Now,' I concluded, 'we have only to wait for a law of a deeper and more far-reaching kind than world history has ever known: the law against treasonous thoughts and emotions. It may be rather a long wait – but it's a law that will surely come.'

She did not seem to react to my feeler. I decided to try the same words that had worked on Karrek.

'Anyone can be caught by that law,' I said meaningfully, adding only after a very long pause: 'I mean, of course – anyone who is not fully loyal through and through.'

Lavris sat silent and thoughtful. The skin over her cheek-bones tautened perhaps a shade more, and suddenly she extended a long, well-formed hand, carefully picked up a pencil between her index finger and thumb, slowly clenching it until her knuckles were white. Without releasing her grip, she looked up again and asked:

'Is that all you have come to see me about, Fellow Soldier?'

'Yes, it is,' I replied. 'Simply to direct the Seventh Bureau's attention to a discovery that may make it possible to show reprehensible inner division, even if division has not yet become a crime in the eyes of the law. If I have taken up the Bureau's time for nothing, I am willing to apologize.'

'The Seventh Bureau thanks you for your good intentions,' she answered with ice-cold impenetrability.

I saluted and left, full of doubt and still glowing with fever.

As I staggered into the Third Bureau with my lists of names, the bell droned the end of the working day and I was nearly knocked over by people rushing out. An ageing, sour-looking man still sat finishing some calculations, and I saw no alternative but to turn to him. He wrinkled his nose, kept his sour mood in check when he saw the recommendations, surveyed the lists and said:

'One thousand, two hundred names, you say? All scientifically meritorious? Pity they're too late. Your request has been granted before you've even had time to present it. The same request came to us from no less than seven other chemistry cities, some eight months ago. Propaganda of the kind you want is already being put together and is well underway.'

'Nothing could please me more,' I said, slightly disappointed at not being able to take part in the meritorious action.

'So there's nothing for you here,' said the man, bowing his head over his columns of figures.

'But would it not be possible for me to take part in some way?' I cried, seized by a bravado that must have been caused by the fever. 'As I demonstrably have such an interest in the matter, why should I not be allowed to take part in the preparations? I have masses of recommendations – look here – and here – and here . . .'

He peered now at my impressive documents, now at his unwritten column; at last he stared with a sigh at the last of his office colleagues who were vanishing out through the doorway. To turn me away he did not dare. At last he chose the solution that seemed to him the one that would waste the least time.

'I'll give you a certificate,' he said, typed out a few lines, quickly took a large rubber stamp, that of the Third Bureau, pressed it below what he had written, and handed me the paper.

'Film Studio Palace at eight o'clock this evening,' he said. 'I don't know what they've got on, but there's always something. It will be all right. No one knows who I am, but they'll recognize the stamp. So, are you satisfied now? I only hope I haven't done something stupid . . .'

CHAPTER 11

I am almost certain that what he had done was something stupid. Only a few days later it became quite clear to me that I
should never really have gained admission to the Film Studio
Palace. It was plain that a different disposition, perhaps a completely different education would have been required were I to
have avoided the shock I now received, and consequently I was
also certain that the right authority would have resolutely
refused me entrance. To be sure, my impressions were probably also distorted by my feverish condition; but distortions of
that kind usually pass rather quickly, and the jolt I experienced
from the evening at the Film Studio Palace left traces behind
for weeks.

My resolute higher existence in the world of principles was of
short duration. Lavris's impenetrable froideur drained my confidence, perhaps first and foremost my belief in myself. Who
was I to put forward plans to save the State? A sick and weary
person, far too sick and weary to have the strength to seek my
refuge among impeccably functioning ethical principles with a
high and toneless voice. Lavris should have had a deep, motherly
voice like that woman from the sect of fools, she should have
comforted me as Linda would have done, she should have been
a completely ordinary and friendly woman . . . Having got that
far, I jerked up from my weary semi-slumber and rushed out of
the metro at the right station. The late-working official's certificate served as a permit, and without really knowing how, I
found myself standing before the underground entrance that
led to the Film Studio Palace. In the capital every building of
importance had an underground entrance, and so it was that

during the whole of my trip to the city I never once happened to come up into the open air.

In pursuing my fancy and asking to take part in some way, it had been with the idea that I might be able to see a film being made. It would have been highly interesting and also, given my state of mind, less stressful to sit more or less comfortably as a spectator, watching how a film scene was created. But I had miscalculated. The room to which I was admitted was an ordinary lecture hall: no floodlights, no backdrops, no costumes were visible, a hundred or so listeners in ordinary leisure uniform filled the seats, that was all. I was questioned in detail about who I was, had all my documents examined, and was at last seated in one of the rows at the very back.

The speeches of welcome were in progress. I was able to work out that what was going on here was an examination in very rough outline of a collection of film scripts that had been delivered; the idea was to draw up the guidelines for a desirable project and to carry out a preliminary selection process. A number of institutions were mentioned as being represented here, including some of the Ministry of Propaganda's bureaux, the Artists' Advisory Committee and the Ministry of Health. On the other hand, the Voluntary Sacrifice Service was not represented, which no one could understand better than I. The principal focus was on the invited lecturer – a psychological specialist in the subject, apparently, and he was being welcomed. As he mounted the speaker's platform I stared at him with curiosity. Psychologists were practically unknown in Chemistry City, except for a few counsellors at the children's and youth camps and the psycho-technicians who conducted the necessary tests when the young people were classified according to the various professions. Djin Kakumita was small and slim of stature, with shiny black hair and very well-considered hand gestures. In attempting to reproduce his introduction to the discussion word for word, I am very well aware that it is impossible, and that long stretches have been lost in my memory. Yet I think that the general picture is still clear enough for me to be able to give an idea of the main gist of the arguments.

'Fellow Soldiers,' he began. 'Before me I have a thick tome that owes its origins to no less than three-hundred-and-seventy-two film script writers. It would be impossible to give an account of each and every one of the three-hundred-and-seventy-two manuscripts in my introduction, and the authors who may be affected must forgive me.' (Laughter among the audience: of course none of these underlings, the writers who had delivered the raw material, had been invited to part in the preparation of the finished text.) 'Instead, I must very quickly draw up a general critique, which at the same time will be a set of guidelines for the project.

'First and foremost I have taken the liberty of dividing these stories into two large main groups: those with a "happy" ending and those with an "unhappy" one. As the aim is to attract and encourage, it might be thought that stories with a happy ending would be best suited to our purpose. Such, however, is not the case – as I shall now demonstrate. What kind of person is attracted by a happy ending? One who is slow to react, one who really, deep down, fears suffering and death – and they are not the people we are addressing. Psychological studies have shown that the Voluntary Sacrifice Service acquires few recruits from them. When such people get to the happy ending they gladly forget what the film was all about. They go home and sleep as soundly as dormice in the assurance that now both hero and heroine are safe. They do not go to the propaganda office to turn themselves in. Voluntary Sacrifice films with a happy ending are made for the interim period between the campaigns, not the campaigns themselves. They are made in order to reassure and encourage family members and other fellow soldiers, should they at some point turn their thoughts to children, siblings or associates who have vanished into the Voluntary Sacrifice Service. Such films need to be shown only sporadically, and if they are to have a truly positive effect they should not only have a happy ending but also contain strong elements of sunny humour, and droll escapades. They should have moving scenes, but not scenes that are heroic. In this respect a number of the manuscripts land between two stools: they are an unsuccessful blend of desirable interim period mentality with the mentality that ought to prevail during the campaign.

'The films that have proved to be most effective have always been the ones with so-called unhappy endings. I say so-called, as what may be viewed as the greatest happiness for the individual is always a matter of discretion – discretion and indifference, as strictly speaking nothing should be seen from the point of view of the individual. At any rate, I allude to films where the hero is defeated. We can always reckon on a certain percentage of fellow soldiers for whom, at root, this appears to be the greatest happiness, and especially if it happens for the State. It's from this percentage that the Voluntary Sacrifice Service acquires most of its recruits, and I have reason to believe – a reason I shall return to later – that in our time it represents a rather high figure. Thus, it is merely a question of arousing and encouraging tendencies that already exist, and of pushing them in the right direction.

'As a rule, however, the future heroes are rather pernickety in their choice of defeat. They want to portray someone who captivates. Above all, they must studiously avoid any illnesses and types of death that possess any laughable characteristics. Conditions in which the test subject becomes a piece of flotsam, unable to preserve his dignity, unable to control himself, unable to manage the most elementary biological needs, are to be avoided when it comes to films of this kind. For films of the interim period – yes, of course! And then with a happy ending and an emphasis on the comical aspect. But the sufferings that lure heroes must be a) *dignified* in appearance, and also b) *expedient*.

'The yearning to feel that one is exclusively an instrument for a higher purpose is a driving force to be reckoned with far beyond the limits of the heroic type I have so far been discussing. As a rule, no one can seriously believe that his life has a value in itself, as such. If we are to speak of the value of a life, it must clearly be a value for something that lies beyond the individual. What day, what hour of our lives do we dare to perceive as a value in itself? Not one. And I would assert that this insight into the worthlessness of the individual life has its counterpart in an ever more powerful awareness of the all-overshadowing demands of the Higher Purpose, in other words the dawning of State consciousness in the brains of the fellow soldiers. The suffering the film portrays must therefore have as its fruit a demonstrably hyper-individual advantage – it must not be one person who is saved by the hero's defeat, for then the person could have saved himself! – nor even a small number of people, but thousands, millions, *preferably all the fellow soldiers in the World State.*

'A subsidiary element of this expediency is c) the *honourable nature* of the defeat that is portrayed. By this I do not mean that the hero should reap positive honour; that would lower the film's level and instantly have a weaker effect on those whose natures are heroic, in the true sense of the word. No, he should be spared deep inner ignominy. For against the hero one pits the villain, who is asocial and has selfish motives, the man who falls to temptation and seeks to avoid pain and death. Downright ugly or unsympathetically sleek in appearance, slouching and undisciplined, cowardly and libidinous, he ought constantly to go through the action like a warning parallel, yet never portrayed more negatively than as a thorn which pricks the sensitive conscience: but you are not like him, are you? In fact, the fear of being cowardly, dishonourable, ugly in the inner sense of the word, is often a strong driving force in the heroic type I have described and which we must make the primary target of our propaganda campaign.

'Very few of the manuscripts I have before me fulfil all the strict requirements I have mentioned. Our work as we continue will certainly be instructive: the material will be divided between a number of studio departments, sorted and criticized according to the guidelines I have drawn up, and whatever can be used will be kneaded together, improved and polished until what remains is a relatively small number of proposals, but all perfectly satisfactory. This work should be complete in two weeks' time, and then we shall meet again and begin to scrutinize the result together. Thank you, and I hope we shall have a lively discussion.'

He stepped down from the speaker's platform. I felt uneasy,

though I could not really say why. I was sure that everyone around me found it reassuring that he spoke of the fellow soldiers in the same way that a skilful technician speaks of ingeniously functioning mechanisms, I was sure that they were carried along by his superiority and felt that they themselves stood in his place above the machine, handling the controls. But whether it was caused by the fever or not, I had an all too lively memory of my first test subject, No. 135, and of his one great moment, which I had envied him. I could despise No. 135 as much as I wanted, I could treat him as badly as I liked in my thoughts or in reality, but as long as I envied him I could never view him in the way that the engineer views his machine.

The discussion began. Someone pointed out the importance of making the heroes of most films young, in order to bring young people aboard. Not because it was so much more *desirable* to have younger sacrifice servants than older ones. Statistics showed that a sacrifice servant lasted on average so-and-so many years, regardless of the age at which he began to be employed, and it could even be said that there was nothing but advantage to be had from the fact that the State *first* got several years of work in a different capacity and *then* this statistical average of years in the Sacrifice Service, instead of *only* these later years. But another reason carried more weight: the young were so much easier to influence. As a rule, marriage and a busy working life had a negative effect on the number of registrations. Of course within all groups and age brackets there were also lone wolves who hungered for they knew not really what, and when so-called 'happiness' and so-called 'life' had left them disappointed they were ready to seek the opposite of those things in the hope that they might have better luck there, and they should not be forgotten. But adolescence – especially a well-managed adolescence – was none the less the age of loneliness and disappointment above all else – or perhaps merely the age of *adventurous* loneliness and disappointment? – and consequently adolescents should receive the primary focus.

Someone else underlined the last speaker's remarks, and added that youth had yet one more advantage over adulthood: since such large numbers of registrations streamed in from the

youth camps after every properly managed propaganda campaign, one could also afford to cream off the best. For it was
senseless to accept each and every one of the registrants without distinction. Many were so gifted that the State would gain
more benefit from their brains than from their tissues and
other body parts. As another consequence of this, the minimum age should not be set too low. Before the age of fifteen or
sixteen it was often hard to judge the general and particular
usability of these registrants.

One speaker with extreme views raised objections to what
this last person had said, and declared that when a child was
only eight years old it was possible to tell if it was specially
gifted and worthy of being singled out, and so the minimum
age for registrations could easily be lowered to eight, and why
not make a few films especially designed to influence that age
group. Against him others in their turn objected partly that
there were many examples of gifted registrants who were of
great use but who did not emerge until a somewhat later point
in time; and partly that such an appeal to child registrants
would not have enough importance to justify the cost of extra
film-making. While it was true that some savings would be
made through the fact that the children who might register
would never need any education, on the other hand it was not
until puberty that heroic inclinations *of this kind* emerged in
earnest.

Another began to speak of how vital it was not to release the
films at intervals that were too far apart. No pressure should
be exerted in order to stimulate these registrations, nor was it
required. A certain element of surprise was sufficient to produce an effect almost as powerful as physical force, and in the
long term much less dangerous. A quick decision needed to be
made: now or never – if it was not done within such and such
a time, it was too late! The fear that usually awoke at certain
times of crisis in one's life was rendered more acute in the face
of rapid choice and drove the person in the right direction, if
the propaganda was well presented.

Someone thanked the last speaker for this insight and
emphasized that this fear, which now and again grew within

every fellow soldier, could be an invaluable asset to the State if experienced psychologists took a hand in it. When it was used, so to speak, as the trigger for a decision, it did no harm at all if the decision was made to seem somewhat momentous. That increased the relief once it was taken, and the ecstatic joy among the first registrants impelled more registrants to sign up in far greater numbers than if the whole affair had been made a trivial matter. To make the decision to join up an irrevocable one was to overshoot the mark, and the speaker considered that even the now obligatory ten years were too much. Exactly the same effect could be obtained with fewer problems if the period of service was made to be five years. Even after five years the sacrifice servant very rarely still had the youth, strength and opportunities to make the transition to a new career. Thanks to well-presented propaganda, all compulsion, and thus all resistance, could be avoided.

Remember that I was ill. No other cause can explain why I stood up and asked for the floor. Strangely enough, No. 135 had not ceased to haunt my heated brain. When I had him under my control I had done everything to humiliate him, but now I felt that I must speak on his behalf:

'I must direct a comment against your treatment of your fellow soldiers – as machines,' I said, slowly and hesitantly. 'It strikes me as an expression of – a lack of esteem – of respect . . .'

My voice failed me, and I noticed that I was too lightheaded to be able to put my words together properly.

'Not at all!' cried one of the previous speakers, sharply and impatiently. 'What insinuations are these? No one could place a higher value on the heroic type than I do. Do you think I don't know how essential it is to the State – I, who have devoted many years of my life to the study of precisely that type and its background? Do you think I did so because I thought it worthless? And then you come here and talk about lack of respect!'

'Yes, yes,' I cried in confusion, 'respect for the result – but – but . . .'

'But what?' asked my antagonist, when I was silent. 'What is it I lack respect for?'

'Nothing,' I replied, feebly, and sat down. 'You are right. I was mistaken, and I apologize.'

I had stopped myself at the right moment, I thought, with sweat on my forehead. What had I meant to say? 'You lack respect for No. 135 himself'? A nice point of view. Secret individualistic tendencies beneath the surface. I was afraid of myself.

No, not myself! It was not me, this thing that I loathed and struggled against. It was not me. It was Rissen.

For a long time I heard nothing of what was taking place around me, so shaken was I by the danger I had escaped. When I finally managed to concentrate, Djin Kakumita stood on the speaker's platform. As far as I could gather, he had already been speaking for a long time.

'With every day that passes this, so to speak, passive heroic type,' he said, 'is becoming more and more sought after in the life of the State. It is essential not only in the Voluntary Sacrifice Service, but also as the ordinary man or woman in the rank and file, the official in a subordinate post, the bearer and supplier of children to the State, and a thousand other positions. The need for it becomes especially strong in wartime, when each and every fellow soldier should belong to this group. On the other hand, it will be clear to anyone that it is not desirable in a position of leadership, where a cold and objective gaze, swift enterprise and ruthless strength are required. Now the problem may be phrased like this: how, if necessary, could we further promote the emergence of this noblest of all types, this desperate and solitary heroic soul, disappointed by life and turned towards suffering and death? Well . . .'

I really felt very unwell, and decided to leave the hall. As I was an outsider and could not therefore belong to any of the work groups, strictly speaking it did not matter. With slow, silent steps, so as to cause the least disturbance, I stole towards the doorway, where I showed the guard my papers and in a whisper began to explain my conduct. While in the process, I was interrupted by a tall, dark-skinned man in military police uniform with rather high rank markings. Oddly enough, he had come in from outside and wished to be admitted to the hall this late in the evening. He showed a document to the

doorman, who not only let him inside at once but also followed him, and I lost no time in stepping out into the corridor.
From within I could hear a low, firm voice, though I was unable
to make out what it was saying, and, when it had finished, a
rising murmur from the audience.

At the same moment, the doorman returned to his place,
and I could not help asking him what was going on.

'Shhh,' he whispered, looking around him. 'Since you heard
it, Fellow Soldier, I will tell you. The making of propaganda
films for the Voluntary Sacrifice Service has been cancelled. All
forces are needed elsewhere. You know what that means, and I
do too, but none of us has the right to know it out loud . . .'

To express oneself was already to know out loud, but I did
not stop to argue, and hurried into the lift, tired as I was. But
he was right: I knew very well what the interruption meant.
The World State lay in the shadow of another war.

CHAPTER 12

My desire for adventure was satisfied. What I had experienced in the capital was varied and instructive enough for me never to forget it: the crucial test of Kallocain in front of Tuareg, my visit to the Seventh Bureau, and last but not least the psychological film discussion, for which I was not ready. No, I was truly not ready for it. It lay within me and gnawed at me like a hidden wound. Yet there was not a single statement to which I had any objection – the purely psychological assertions I had to leave to the professionals in the field – and I felt horribly ashamed each time I thought of my unwarranted and stupid interjection. When I had taken a position, why should it then continue to torment me? Never had I heard stated so clearly, so dispassionately, how in objective terms the value of each fellow soldier's contribution might be considered – and yet it felt as though the effort of existing had become so gigantically enormous and the meaning of it all so vanishingly small. I knew this was a false and unhealthy view of things, and I tried to convince myself with every possible argument. But for the desolate emptiness that opened ever wider within me there was no other name but *meaninglessness*.

It would have served me right, I thought with horror, if some facetious policeman, or maybe Rissen, had taken the syringe out of my hand and stuck it in my own arm instead. What the Seventh Bureau would have said about my state of mind was easy to imagine. Had Rissen only been within his rights, he would probably have been glad to take it upon himself to unmask me, I thought, and find proof of his earlier theorem: 'No fellow soldier over forty has a clear conscience.' Was not that what he had wanted all along? Was it not really he who had led me here with his sneaky insinuations? The man was a danger to me and to everyone else. The most horrible thing of all was to wonder about how far he had led Linda with him into perdition, and whether they were in league against me, both of them.

All of this lay beneath the surface, festering. On the face of it, I had far too much to do to devote my time to rumination. Tuareg had already given orders that the ordinary work of the courts should be replaced with Kallocain-testing, and people from all over the World State were already standing in line to enrol in the new courses we had been told to arrange. We were transferred – temporarily, it was said – to the police service and were given premises in police headquarters. Karrek had all the remand prisoners brought directly to our lecture rooms for the dual purpose of being investigated and of serving as practice material; there was therefore always a higher-ranking military or police officer present as judge, and the records were kept both by police secretaries and whatever secretaries were assigned to the course.

It soon turned out that we were up to our ears in work. We had to admit more people to the courses than was really practical, and yet many others had to wait. Nor could we keep up with all the remand prisoners who arrived; we had to hurry from one case to another, and we even cut our lunch break by half an hour.

After all, the work of the courts had been secret from time immemorial; I therefore had nothing with which to make comparisons. But it struck me that so many of the denunciations were false or at any rate unnecessary. Almost each and every one of the tested subjects stumbled out crushed and broken – without reason, one might almost think, having been hardened by the hundreds of ins and outs in the revelations of more or less eccentric fellow soldiers – and yet what they revealed was often of such a laughably trivial nature, seen from the court's point of view, that one began to wonder if the apparatus was worth its price. There were also difficulties with the supply of Kallocain, which was still being manufactured by the lab only in small quantities.

On one occasion we happened to discuss the issue at the lunch table (we, that is, Rissen, I and all the members of the course, who had managed to book several long tables in the large refectory where the police headquarters auxiliary staff also ate). We had as usual been furiously busy all morning, the air had been even hotter and more humid than usual, and to cap it all some of the fans on our floor had gone on strike. Someone was complaining loudly about all the denunciations that were being made for trivial misdemeanours or for nothing at all.

'The denunciations have been increasing steadily during the past twenty years,' said Rissen. 'I have it on the authority of the chief of police himself.'

'But it doesn't mean that criminality has increased,' I said. 'It may equally be loyalty that has increased, there's more awareness of what's rotten . . .'

'It means that terror has increased,' said Rissen, with unexpected vehemence.

'Terror?'

'Yes, terror. We've been moving towards ever stricter surveillance – and it hasn't made us safer, as we hoped, but more fearful. Along with our terror grows our impulse to strike out around us. Isn't it so: when a wild animal feels threatened and sees no way to flee and escape, it goes on the attack. When terror creeps over us, there is nothing left to do but to strike the first blow. It's hard, as we don't even know where to strike the blow . . . An ounce of prevention is worth a pound of cure, the old adage says, doesn't it? If one strikes with enough frequency and enough skill, one may perhaps save oneself. There's an old humorous tale about a fencer who was so adept that he managed to stay dry when it rained: he swung his sword at the drops as they fell, so that none of them landed on him. In somewhat similar fashion must we fence, we who have ended up in the great terror.'

'You talk as though everyone had something to hide,' I said, but I could hear how lame it sounded, how lacking in conviction. Although I did not want to believe him, against my will I saw a scene that frightened me. *If* he was right, if my errand with Lavris bore fruit, if not only words and actions but also thoughts and feelings were to be investigated and judged – then, then . . . Like crawling ants on an anthill all the fellow soldiers would start to move, but not in order to co-operate, like ants, but to get ahead of one another. I saw them swarming: work colleagues denouncing work colleagues, husbands denouncing wives and wives denouncing husbands, subordinates denouncing chiefs and chiefs denouncing subordinates . . . It was out of the question for Rissen to be right. I hated him for having the power to force his thoughts on me. But I grew calm when I thought of who would be the first to be denounced, if the new law became a reality.

A few days later an order came from Karrek that the course was to be split up. The continued investigations, plus appropriate training, would be led by Rissen, with the assistance of the most advanced students. I, on the other hand, was to lead a special chemistry course, so that the manufacture of Kallocain could be started on a larger scale.

The matter was urgent, I realized that. Moreover, I ought to have been pleased to be able to go back to chemistry again. And yet the order made me annoyed and disappointed.

Among our test subjects we had always had the same ageing man from the sect of fools whom I mentioned earlier and who had come in before our trip to the capital. By chance, his case had been postponed – he had fallen ill and not recovered until now – and he was on the schedule for tomorrow, the very day I was to begin my new chemistry course. It surprised and almost frightened me that I was so disappointed not to be able to attend that interrogation. I could not help wondering if I was expecting something in the style of that woman who had made such a deep impression on me – if I was being drawn to expose myself to similar dangerous influences again. But I did not really need immediately to look for derogatory motives. My interest lay first and foremost with the whole of the tangle that Karrek had ordered us to unravel – I wanted to know what the nucleus was that lay concealed behind all the craziness. The man's intelligent appearance indicated that he might be more deeply cognizant with the junta's innermost secrets than anyone we had encountered so far. Interest may also be of a negative kind, I told myself, one that has nothing positive about it. Such was my interest in the sect of fools, just like my interest in Rissen.

Even though I was compelled to obey orders, I promised myself that I would not let the case completely drop out of view.

'Is one permitted to ask if that ill man was questioned today?' I asked the following day, at lunch.

'Yes, he was examined today,' Rissen replied, curtly.

'And what emerged? Anything criminal?'

'He was sentenced to penal labour.'

'For what?'

'He was considered to be treasonous.'

It was impossible to get anything firm and tangible out of my control chief. I saw no other way out but to ask to see the record.

'That I have no authority to allow or forbid,' said Rissen. 'It's a matter for the chief of police.'

Karrek raised no difficulties when I asked him on the phone. So on my first night off I went up to police headquarters, where Rissen was waiting for me. He unlocked the cabinet and handed me the document. It was the course report (the police report was somewhere else, I don't know where) and rather extensive. I had to read it on the spot, and at first it bothered me that Rissen had work to do there precisely on that evening. I realized that he wished to give me explanations and clarifications, and I did not want them.

But after I had begun my reading, I changed my mind. As he was within earshot, I thought I might as well ask him.

'There is something here that I would like more details about,' I said. '"The subject began to sing strange songs." What's meant by that? Why were they strange?'

Rissen shrugged.

'They just were,' he answered. 'They were like nothing I have ever heard. Obscure words, just similes and images, I think – and melodies, though I don't know how any soldiers in the world would be able to march in time with them . . . But they made a deep impression on me, and seldom has anything affected me like that.'

His voice was shaking so noticeably that his emotion began to affect me, too. I should never have come here. I should have been warned by that warm female voice that spoke of the organic and afterwards always floated in my mind like the deepest of all repose. The voice suddenly came to life for me again, and it struck me as something almost unjust, insidious and demonic that an inner contagion could transplant itself, not only into one's own mind but also into the minds of others – from the strange man, whose I singing I had not heard, and to me, like an echo over Rissen's voice.

'Can you give me some idea of his songs?' I asked, unsteadily. 'Can you sing them?'

But he shook his head.

'It was too strange. It just drugged me.'

I went on reading and made an effort to get away from this influence, which I hated.

'You must admit that this is criminal,' I said. 'As far as I'm aware, the release of all geographical information and rumours is punishable by law. And this: "A deserted city of ruins in an inaccessible location"! I see that he wasn't able to give the precise location, but was merely intent on spreading insinuations of that kind!'

'Who can tell if it exists, that desert city?' Rissen replied, hesitantly. 'He himself maintained that it was known only to a chosen few, that there were some of them who lived among the ruins. Why does it need to be anything more than a story?'

'A criminal story, in that case, as it's nonetheless a geographical rumour. If such a desert city existed, and if, as he says, it derived from the time before the great wars and before the World State, and if it really was destroyed with bombs and gas and bacteria – then how could anyone dare to live there, even if they were fools? If it were possible for human life to exist there, the State would have taken it over long ago.'

'If you look a bit further on in the report,' Rissen replied, 'you will see that it says that the city is still full of dangers; it says that in some places the very stone and sand are mixed with poisonous vapours, that in cracks and crevices swarms of bacteria have managed to survive, and in general there is danger every step of the way. But as you will also see, he says that there are arteries of fresh water in the ground, that there is uncontaminated soil suitable for growing edible plants, that the few inhabitants know the roads and hiding places that are safe, and live in friendship and mutual assistance.'

'I'm looking, I'm looking. A wretched and insecure life, full of fear. But it's an instructive tale. That is what life must be like, in constant fear and danger, when one tries to flee the great uniting principle, the State.'

He was silent. I continued to read, and could not help sighing and shaking my head.

'A tale!' I said. 'A fairy tale about something that doesn't exist! The remains of a dead culture! In that gas-polluted desert hole they are said to have preserved the remains of a dead culture from the time before the great wars! There was no such culture.'

Rissen turned towards me quickly.

'How can you be so sure of that?' he asked.

I stared at him in surprise.

'But that is something we learned when we were children,' I said. 'Nothing that was worth the name "culture" can be thought to have existed during the civilian-individualist era. Individuals fought individuals, social groups fought social groups. Valuable energies, strong arms, excellent brains could be arbitrarily uncoupled, hurled aside by an adversary, locked out of the work force, to waste away unused and without purpose . . . That is what I would call a jungle, not culture.'

'So would I,' Rissen agreed, earnestly. 'And yet, and yet . . . isn't it possible to imagine a spring, an underground spring, ebbing, overlooked, that broke into the daylight even in the jungle?'

'Culture is the life of the State,' I replied, curtly. But his words set my imagination in motion. As I sat there hunched over the report, I had seen myself as a kind of superior and adjudicating critic. In reality, my greedy imagination was searching in the most remote, the most unknown regions for something that could deliver me from the present, or give me a key with which to unlock it. But I did not understand that.

One part of the report really made me sit up. The man had described a tradition according to which at one time tribes on the other side of the border were said to have belonged to certain border peoples in the World State. The area was said to have been split in two during the great wars, and the people likewise.

I looked up.

'That is too much, that bit about the border peoples,' I said in a voice that shook with righteous anger. 'It's both immoral and unscientific.'

'Unscientific?' he repeated, almost absently.

'Yes, unscientific! Are you not aware, my chief, that nowadays our biologists consider it fully proven that we here in the World State and those creatures on the other side of the border are quite simply descended from different species of apes, as different as night and day, and so unlike each other that one may very well wonder if the "peoples" of the neighbour state should be called people at all.'

'I'm not a biologist,' he replied, evasively. 'I haven't heard that before.'

'Then I'm glad to have had the opportunity of talking about it. For that is how it is. And that it's an immoral tradition I don't think I need to explain any further. You can imagine the consequences of a border war. The question is whether that entire sect of fools, with its teachings, customs and attitude to life, is another stage in the neighbour state's attempts to undermine our security – one detail of many in the enormous spying apparatus it seems to have at its disposal.'

Rissen was silent for a long time, and finally said:

'It was mostly because of that tradition that he was sentenced.'

'I'm only surprised that he wasn't sentenced to death.'

'He was a skilled professional in a branch of dye-making, where there seems to be a staff shortage.'

I made no reply. I knew that his sympathies lay on the side of the criminal. But I could not resist giving him a little prod:

'Well, my chief – aren't you glad that we've finally got to the heart of the matter and know where to put our dear sect of fools?'

'I suppose it's a loyal fellow soldier's duty to be glad,' he said with an irony I was perhaps not supposed to notice. 'And if I may ask a question in return, Fellow Soldier Kall: are you quite sure that deep down you don't envy them their gas-filled desert city?'

'That doesn't exist, yes,' I replied, laughing. Was Rissen in his right mind? If it was a joke, it was a bad one, with no sting in its tail.

Yet his question was to torment me for a long time, as so many of his words tormented me, as the emotional trembling of his voice tormented me, as the whole of Rissen, that ridiculous, sly and civil man tormented me.

With all my might I rejected the idea of the Desert City, perhaps less because it was impossible than because it was repellent. At once repellent and attractive. It went against my better sense to believe in the existence of a city, even if it lay in ruins, even if it gaped with the perils of gas and bacteria, even if the asocial individuals who sought their miserable refuge there crept among the stones harried by fear and terror, and now and then fell victim to a lurking death – but still a city where the power of the State did not reach, an area outside the community. The attractive element in the idea – who could say what it was? Superstition is often attractive, I thought with disdain. It is a casket where one keeps one's lurking temptations like jewels; a deep female voice; a tremor in a man's voice; a moment one has never experienced, of complete devotion; a reprehensible dream of personal trust without limits; a hope of quenched thirst and profound repose.

At any rate I was unable to defend myself against my own curiosity. I did not really dare to ask Rissen about the subsequent fate of the sect of fools, from which I myself was locked out, as I was afraid that he would read into my questions a different and more positive interest than I really had. All I dared to do was make ironic comments at the lunch table. To these he also gave short, ill-tempered answers. For example, I said:

'That extremely dubious Desert City – it's still on the moon, I suppose? It hasn't acquired an earthly existence?'

And he replied:

'So far, at least, no one has been able to specify its location.'

On quickly looking up, I met his eyes for a second. He at once lowered them again, but I had time to read a question in them, and I could feel it drilling its way in: 'Are you quite sure that deep down you don't envy them their gas-filled desert city?' He would all too willingly have attributed to me an envy of that kind. Although he was forcing me to take the initiative, it was he who was the attacker, trying to harass me into submission. I cursed my morbid curiosity.

I was able to glean one more piece of information, this time not from Rissen but from a female student, even without asking. She was saying something about collections of writing, which one of the remand prisoners had talked about – thick volumes of documents that contained signs that were said to represent musical notes, but did not at all resemble our conventional notation. They almost made one think of the bodies of birds behind the bars of a cage, apparently. No one could decipher them, not even the furtive inhabitants of the desert city, though they must have had immense collections from ages long past. I was quite certain that if there were music in all those signs – it might all equally well be a hoax – it must be music of a primitive and barbarous kind. Yet I had an almost uncontrollable longing to hear them performed – a stupid dream that would probably never be fulfilled, either for me or for anyone else. And even if it were, there could not possibly be any meaning in what must be a collection of military marches, so how would there be any help in them, or any solution to a problem?

Meanwhile my life at home was dull and empty. Linda and I had drifted so far apart that it was no longer worth making the effort to communicate. Luckily we were both so busy that we rarely met.

CHAPTER 13

Some time later, on my night off, I was summoned to see Karrek.

As I sat in the metro with my visitor's permit in my pocket, I heaved a sigh of relief. Karrek was and remained one of the points of support for my existence. In him there was none of the morbid contagion that frightened me in Rissen and caused my antagonism.

Karrek received me in the parents' room, while his wife sat reading by a small nightlight in the family room. (They had no children.) The lighting where we were was also rather dim – this had become increasingly common of late, for reasons of economy – so that I was unable to study the police chief's features in any detail, but in his movements I noticed something unusual that disturbed me, though I could not work out what it was. Hardly for one moment was he still; now he sat down, now he stood up again, measuring the floor with strides that were far too long for the meagre space. When the wall impeded his progress he would sometimes rap his knuckles impatiently on it, as if to push away the hindrance.

When he began to speak, I noticed the same unusual liveliness in his voice; it was exalted, almost euphoric, and he scarcely bothered to conceal his state of mind.

'Well now, what do you say?' he began. 'We've succeeded, you and I. Lavris must have induced Ta Cho to issue that law against treasonous thinking. It comes into force tomorrow. Then – yes, then it will begin.'

For a moment I felt paralysed by the fact that it had actually happened and that the fateful day was so near. It clearly made him nothing but cheerful. My lips, on the other hand, trembled, and I had to pull myself together as I replied:

'I wonder if this was really a good idea, my chief? Sometimes I wish we hadn't done it. Don't misunderstand me, my reasons are purely practical. To me at least it seems as though there is already enough dirt to rummage about in, more than the State can afford, even. We're already working overtime. Well, it can be put right just as soon as we've trained some assistants. But what is to be done with all the new denunciations? We can't have two-thirds of the population doing penal labour!'

'Why not?' he said cheerfully, clenching his fist at the wall. 'It won't make much difference, and the budget for salaries will be smaller. But seriously, there have been complaints from the Head of Finance in the city, and this seems to be the same everywhere else, too. It means that for financial reasons we shall have to be more selective about denunciations. In future, no one will be arrested unless the informer makes a detailed written account of the reasons for his suspicions. That in itself will start the weeding-out. What's more, we shall only devote our attention to the more eminent fellow soldiers. We must focus all our attention on the security of the State, you understand. Subordinate positions must be scrutinized with a fine-tooth comb at some point in the future, and crimes like robbery, theft and minor private homicide come last. We must weed, weed, and weed, but don't worry, we shall have plenty of work to do.'

Karrek resumed his pacing and burst into laughter, the short, shrill neigh that was so typical of him.

'No one will find it easy to escape,' he said.

Just then he stood in such a way that the light from the lamp glittered in his eyes. A face lit up from below often looks terrifying, and I happened to be in a time of overstrain in my life. The fact is that when I saw the gleam in his jaguar eyes, my blood ran cold – they were so horribly near and at the same time so horribly far, utterly out of reach, resting in their own chill. Mainly to calm myself, I retorted quietly:

'I suppose what you really mean is that everyone will have a bad conscience?'

'Bad conscience?' he repeated, and neighed again. 'What

does it matter if they have a good or a bad conscience? Even if they're as cool and collected as cucumbers – no one will find it easy to escape!'

'Escape denunciation, you mean?'

'Denunciation and conviction are what I mean. You see – sit down, by all means sit down, Fellow Soldier – you see' (here he approached again, leaning over me, and I was all too glad to sink down in a chair, so badly were my knees shaking), *it's a matter of having the right advisers and the right judge.* We get judges from different places, you see, specialists in different areas, and stupid sentences should not be given, as you'll appreciate: a confirmed criminal should not be sent for rehabilitation, and in these days of declining birth rates one should not rob the State of the work potential of those who are soft in the head and have slightly outdated ideas. But, as I say, the field is open for the man who knows what he wants. Everything is possible if one has the right judge.'

I must admit that I did not really understand what he meant. But neither did I want to tell him that. So I nodded earnestly, and watched his pacing across the floor with a gaze of some alarm.

The silence in the room now felt awkward. I supposed that the police chief expected me to say something. His words about different sentences awoke the memory of something I really had planned to say to him.

'My chief,' I said, 'there is a matter that has rather surprised me. They had a man here being injected the other day, a conspirator who belonged to the dangerous sect of fools. He not only spread geographical rumours of an extremely harmful nature but also a monstrous story about the beings on the other side of the border sharing the same origin as some of our border tribes. He also sang asocial songs. He was sentenced to penal labour. Now I wonder: it may well be that this was the right punishment in his particular case – the case is closed, and I am certainly not criticizing the judgement – but is it a good idea, purely from the point of view of principle? As one may imagine, during his term of penal labour a prisoner comes into contact with a great many people, both prison guards and other prisoners. Of the prisoners, some are only in custody for a short time, others for longer, but many are eventually released. Must one not consider the poison to which they are exposed from a person of that type? It may not be possible for that person to say very much, that's true. But I have made a discovery. I beg you, my chief, please don't laugh at me – but I have noticed that from some people there radiates such a very strong sensation of the whole of their attitude to life that they are dangerous even when they say nothing. One glance, one movement from such an individual is already poison and plague. Now I wonder: is it a good idea to let such an individual live? Even if he can be employed for useful labour, and even if our birth-rate is falling, is it not more likely that he will harm the State with his very breathing than benefit it with his labour?'

Karrek did not laugh. He listened carefully and showed no surprise. When I had finished, a gleam of sly amusement spread across his face, he stopped his pacing and sank down on the chair facing mine. There he sat, with another leap stored up in his tense immobility.

'You need not beat about the bush, dear Fellow Soldier,' he said, softly and slowly. 'No one is more willing than I to deplore the gloomy fact to which you allude: that a very large group of fellow soldiers has acquired a wholly inappropriate value merely because the birth-rate is not rising fast enough. All the propaganda we daily bring to life is not sufficient to improve our performance in the marital bed to the required extent. But what can you or I do about it? Put general points of principle aside. Behind them always lies the individual case. So, who is it you want condemned to death?'

I wished I could sink through the floor. His cynicism alarmed me. It was of course not only Rissen I had been talking about, but the problem as a whole. Who did he really think I was?

'You did me a great service when you convinced Lavris,' he continued. 'One good turn deserves another, that's how one knows the people one can count as friends. You appear to have a certain sort of intelligence, or at any rate one of a completely different sort than mine' (here he broke into a neigh again). 'So we can be of use to each other. You may answer my question with a calm mind: who is it that you want condemned to death?'

But I could not answer. Until now my wishes had been only wishes, unreal and floating freely in the air. I felt that I must see them for myself in a sober light once again, before I acted.

'No, no,' I replied, 'my misgivings are really of a general nature, on principle. I have experience of such plague carriers.'

I stopped myself. Had I said too much? For a few more seconds he still sat motionless, and I squirmed under his green eyes. Then he got up again and punched the wall with his knuckles.

'You don't want to. You're afraid of me. And I have nothing against that. But I will do what I can for you. When you send in your denunciation – or denunciations, for all I know – well-motivated ones, mind you, well-motivated, that will be the main requirement from now on, and it is not I who makes the initial selection – put a sign in one corner, this sign' (he drew it on a piece of paper and handed it to me), 'and then I will do what I can. As I said, it's not so tricky at all if one has the right judge, and I think we can arrange that. The right judge and the right advisers. I don't plan to let you go, and you can have great benefit from me – even though you are afraid.'

CHAPTER 14

My sleep had never been the best, but recently it had become really bad. My monthly ration of sleeping pills was always finished long before the middle of the month, and what Linda did not need of hers I used up to the last drop. I did not want to consult a doctor. I suspected that then I would receive the stamp 'nervous constitution' on my secret card, and that would not be pleasant, especially as I myself could not on any terms agree to such a designation. No one could be more normal than I, my sleeplessness was all too natural and explicable, and indeed I would have seen it as sick and unnatural had I been able to sleep well under such circumstances . . .

At all events, my anxiety dreams showed clearly enough that I was not exactly longing to be tested with my own Kallocain. Sometimes I would wake up in a cold sweat from terrible visions in which I stood as an accused man waiting for my dose, and for the dreadful shame that would follow. Rissen, Karrek and even some of the students appeared fleetingly as bogeymen in my dreams, but above all it was Linda. She was always there as my denouncer, my judge, the person who leaned over me with the Kallocain syringe. Initially I would wake up with relief and see the real Linda of flesh and blood beside me in the bed, but soon it was as if the visions of the night began to encroach on waking reality, so that each time the relief grew less and the tangible and waking Linda absorbed more and more of the bogeyman's spite and malice. On one occasion I was close to telling her all about my nightly torture – but held back at the last moment with the memory of her cold gaze in the dream. Afterwards I was glad I had not said anything. The suspicion that Linda was secretly on Rissen's side no longer left me any peace. If she were to find out what I thought of him, she could at that same moment become my enemy, and a merciless enemy, she was that strong. No, if I had said a word to her about this it would have been my undoing.

Even less would I have wanted to tell her about another dream, one that cannot really be counted among the usual nightmares. It was a dream about the Desert City.

I stood at the beginning of a street, and knew that I must go along it – why I did not know, but I was agonizingly certain that my welfare depended on whether I got there. The houses on both sides of the street were heaps of ruins, some as tall as little mountains, others subsided into the ground and half-covered with sand and rubble. In one or two places creeping plants had taken root, aspiring up what remained of walls, but between them long stretches of ground lay bare and lifeless in the burning midday sun. And it seemed to me that here and there on the lifeless stretches the stone exhaled a faint, yellow-ish vapour. In other places the light broke over the sand in a blue, hazy shimmer, which I found just as alarming. I took a step to find my way among the poisonous fumes, but instantly a breath of wind arrived, driving a little cloud of the yellow vapour before it – the cloud spread in thin eddies, and I had to back away in order to avoid coming into contact with it. Fur-ther along the street I also saw that in one place the blue, hazy shimmer was beginning to rise up like a dim flame, almost blocking the entire street. I looked round, fearful that a similar explosion behind me might cut off my return, so that I could go neither forward nor back, but so far there were no signs of it. Again I took a step forward. Nothing happened. Another. But then I heard a sharp little crack behind me, and when I turned my head I saw that the stone I had just stepped on was in the process of being transformed. It disintegrated from within, became porous, and crumbled into dust in a moment, while I thought I could detect a faint, unpleasant smell. I felt I could neither go on, stand still or turn around.

Then I heard strange sounds of voices some distance away. Over there, a semi-collapsed cellar doorway gaped with green creeping plants on both sides. I had not noticed it before, but in my anguish I gave a sigh of relief when I saw the living green leaves so close to me. Up the cracked and sunken stone steps someone emerged into the light and waved to me to approach. I no longer remember how I ended up in the cellar doorway, perhaps I took a wild leap over the dangerous stones. At any rate, I entered a ruined stone chamber with no roof, where the sun fell in and flowers swayed above my head. Never had a room with ceiling and walls intact seemed such a safe place of refuge to me. From the tufts of grass spread a scent of sun and earth and carefree warmth, and the voices still sang, though now at a great distance. The woman who had waved to me was there, and we embraced each other. I was saved, and with tiredness and relief felt the urge to sleep. It had suddenly become quite unnecessary for me to go to the end of the street. She said: 'Will you stay with me?' 'Yes, let me stay!' I replied, and felt free from all worry, like a child. When I stooped down to see what the wetness was that I felt with my foot, I noticed that across the whole of the earthen floor a clear spring flowed, and it filled me with an indescribable gratitude. 'Don't you know that this is where life springs up?' said the woman. At that moment I knew that it was a dream, that I was going wake up from it, and I searched in my thoughts for some means of holding on to it – so eagerly, that my heart began to thump and woke me.

That dream, beautiful though it was, could perhaps be called even more suspect than the anxiety dreams, and I did not want to repeat it, not to Linda or to anyone else. Not because Linda would have been jealous of the woman in my dream – she bore certain features of the woman remand prisoner with the deep voice whom I have already mentioned several times, though she had Linda's eyes – but because it was such a clear answer to Rissen's question: 'Are you sure that you don't envy them their gas-filled desert city?' So deep had Rissen's suggestion penetrated that even my dreams were subject to his influence. What good would it do me if I defended myself by saying that this was not I, but Rissen? No judge in the world would have any time for such a defence.

This happened before I was summoned to Karrek, and thus

before the new law had been issued, and before I had any way of protecting myself other than a vague hope of revenge at some time in the future.

When I left Karrek and knew that tomorrow I would be able to turn my thoughts of revenge into action, I was in a horribly disturbed state of mind. The goal, which before had been so distant, suddenly lay within reach, but all the details connected with attaining it suddenly appeared insuperable. If Linda really loved Rissen, would she not in one way or another get the clear idea that it was I who had informed on him? What she would do I did not know, but I was quite sure that she would succeed. She would succeed, and she would have her revenge. Her revenge made me tremble. Whatever happened, I did not want to end up under my own Kallocain needle.

That night I hardly slept at all.

Next morning the newspaper contained an article with the headline:

THOUGHTS CAN BE PUNISHED

It was an account of the new law, mentioning my Kallocain, which had made it possible. Nothing could sound more reasonable than the new penal provisions: from now on there would be no more compliance with paragraphs fixed like blocks of wood that meted out the same punishment to the hardened criminal as to the first-time offender, if they were caught in the same act. The fellow soldier himself would be the centre of the legal process, not his act perceived in isolation. His mentality would be investigated and registered, not because of the old, meaningless question about whether he was 'responsible for his actions', but in order to distinguish relevant material from material that was irrelevant. The punishment would no longer consist in a certain mechanically allotted number of years of penal labour, but would instead be worked out precisely according to the calculations of the most eminent psychologists and economists as to what was appropriate and what was not. A physical and mental wreck who could never be thought to be of any real advantage to the State, ought not to expect to be allowed to live because he had never succeeded in doing any harm. On the other hand, there was a need to take the low population figures into account, and in the worst case even make use of less desirable material, if it could be used as labour force. The new law against treasonous thinking would go into effect today, but at the same time it was pointed out that all denunciations must be thoroughly motivated and also signed with a verifiable name, and not anonymously as before. This was to prevent a flood of less essential denunciations and consequently a large State expenditure on Kallocain and legal personnel. At any rate, the police reserved the right to accept or reject the denunciations as they thought fit.

The part about having to provide one's name was something that Karrek had not told me. It would make it even easier for Linda, should she want to root out the people who had informed on Rissen.

The workday went by without sensational events, but I cannot say that it passed in peace and quiet. Not a word did I exchange with Rissen; at lunch I scarcely dared to look at him. I had a terrible suspicion that he knew my thoughts and my intentions, and might at any moment take the plunge and forestall me. At the same time I knew I that I did not dare to do anything, as I was not sure of Linda. Each hour's delay was dangerous, but I had no option.

When later, back at home, I sat over my evening meal, it was like a repeat of that awful lunch. The same difficulty in meeting Linda's eyes as, earlier, Rissen's, the same feeling that she must know everything, the same hostility that charged the air between us. The seconds crept on, and I thought the home help would never leave, nor the children go to sleep. At last I was alone with Linda, and to avoid eavesdroppers I put the radio on at full volume and arranged our chairs so that the loudspeaker came between us and the police ear.

I no longer remember the subject of the radio talk that blasted out at us, as I was too absorbed in my inner commotion to notice. Linda did not allow her expression to show anything of what she thought either of the talk or of my eagerness to have her sitting in that particular chair – most probably she realized what was afoot, and was no more listening than I was. Only when I moved my chair up close to hers did she give me an inquiring look.

'Linda!' I said. 'There is something I must ask you about.'

'Yes,' was all she said, showing no surprise. I had always known that she had perfect self-control. And I had always known that if the two of us were ever to reach the last extremity, a struggle for life or death, she would be the most fearsome adversary. Was that the real reason why I could not let her go? Was I afraid of what might happen afterwards? In my very love itself lay the great terror, I knew it now and had long been aware of it. But there was also a dream of security without limit, a dream that one day my stubborn love would compel her to be my ally. How that would happen, and how I would know it had happened, I had no idea – it was a dream as vague and distinct from reality as the dream of a life to come. But what was certain was that at the very next moment I could have lost this dreamed-of security. From uncertain allies we could in the space of a moment have turned into bitter enemies, even without my ever knowing it, without a look on her face or a tremor in her voice betraying her. Yet I had to go on.

'I'm asking this as a pure formality, of course,' I continued, trying to smile. 'I'm certain of the answer, have never for one moment believed anything of the kind, and listen, even if it were true, I wouldn't give a damn about it. You know me that well, I hope – and that is how well I know you.'

I dabbed my forehead with my handkerchief.

'Well?' said Linda, giving me a probing look. Her large eyes were like spotlights, so exposed did I feel when she turned them on me.

'Well – it's just this,' I said (and now I smiled really very cheerfully): 'Have you had a love affair with Rissen?'

'No.'

'But you love him?'

'No, Leo, I don't.'

That was as far as we could go, and no further. Had she said yes, I would have believed her without question – I think. Well, and as she said no, I did not dare to look at her even for a moment. Then what had been the point of asking? She had seen that I was lying, she realized that I cared a great deal about her answer. Tomorrow or the day after she would realize why I had asked her – perhaps she already knew, perhaps Rissen had given her a hint of the danger that threatened him. I stared into her face relentlessly, so that I even forgot to breathe and had to gasp for air. My heart almost stopped beating when I thought I detected a movement, faint, scarcely noticeable, a kind of restlessness in her skin – but a sign nonetheless. I had more faith in that sign than in all her words.

'You don't believe me?' she asked, looking grave.

'Of course I believe you,' I replied effusively. If only she believed me too! Had I been able to lull her into security, it would at least not have made things worse. But I sensed that she would not allow herself to be deceived.

We could get no further. This conversation alone had cost me so much self-control that I was quite exhausted – and yet nothing had been gained. Never before had I felt the gaping chasm so clearly and so insurmountably. My self-control was not sufficient to fill the rest of the evening with pleasantries and everyday chat, and yet it was only a matter of an hour, as we both had night duty. Linda also said nothing, and there was a silent unease between us, one that sucked the marrow from one's bones.

At last that hour, too, was over.

Late at night we both came home, tired out. Linda fell asleep, I could hear her regular breathing, but I lay awake. Now and then I would sink into a semi-slumber, but each time I jumped awake again in a sharp awareness of danger. It could be my imagination, the room was quiet and Linda slept as deeply before. But I was close to desperation. Had no one really ever thought before what a risky venture it was to sleep side by side with someone else, two people alone all the long night, with no witnesses but the police eye and the police ear on the wall – and even they brought no security: for one thing, they were probably not always in use, and for another, while they could certainly monitor and avenge, they could not prevent what happened. Two people alone, night after night year after year, and perhaps they hate each other, and if the wife were to wake up, what might she not inflict on her husband ... Now if Linda had taken Kallocain ...

The thought seized me in the same way as a wave lifts a piece of bark. I no longer had any choice, I had to act as I did, in pure self-defence, to save my life. Somehow it must be possible. I could smuggle out the small amount of Kallocain that was needed, under some pretext. Linda would be forced to give up her secrets.

Then she would be in my power as I had never been in hers. Then she would never dare to harm me. Then I could also go further, and denounce Rissen.

Then I would be free.

CHAPTER 15

I did not sleep much that night, but by the time I presented myself at my work I had shaken off the anxiety and indecision that had weighed on me during the preceding days. I was on the way to action; that in itself was already a liberation.

Nothing was simpler than to abscond with enough Kallocain for an injection. Small quantities always went missing during the experiments, and check-weighing was done comparatively rarely, especially now that urgency had taken priority over proper management. And above all: it was Rissen who did the weighing. As long as he did not have the unfortunate idea of ambushing me today or tomorrow with a check-weighing, he would never again have a chance to perform one. In the general bedlam, the person who was his witness and assistant would surely not think of such a detail. Once tomorrow was over I would be safe. I must rely on my good luck, and on Rissen's haste.

So that evening I arrived home with a syringe in my pocket and a small bottle filled with innocently pale green liquid. And the sense of liberation at having taken the first step to action gave me new energy, so that I even managed to chat and gossip with the home help and the children during the evening meal. To Linda I merely nodded, but without avoiding her eyes. They were spotlights, but not as penetrating as the one I had in my pocket.

There was military duty that evening, and we did not get to bed until late.

For a long time I lay still, waiting for her to fall asleep. When at last I was sure, I crept up to the police eye by the glow of the little nightlight and blocked it with a cloth and a pillow, as unabashedly as I had seen Karrek do it. It was forbidden, of course, but I was on the verge of desperation, and whatever happened I did not want to let the police observe my activities.

As Linda lay there in the dim lighting, I had seldom seen her so beautiful. With her naked, gold-shimmering arm she had drawn the coverlet up to her chin, as if she were trying to protect herself from the chill, although the room was very warm. She had twisted her head to one side, so that her regular profile was clearly visible against the shadows on the pillow; her skin glowed like smooth, living velvet against her heavy black eyebrows and eyelashes. The taut red bow of her mouth had relaxed in sleep to the soft and very tired lips of a girl. I had never seen her look so young when awake, not even when we were first becoming acquainted with each other, and never so emotionally affecting. Though I was usually so afraid of her because of her strength, I was almost seized by compassion for her helpless, childlike weakness. The Linda who now lay there before me I would have liked to approach in a different way, tenderly and carefully as if it were the first time we had met. But I knew that if I woke her, the red bow would tauten and the eyes turn into spotlights again. She would sit up straight and wide-awake in bed and with a frown discover the cloth and the pillow on the wall. And what if I still wanted to approach her, if I brought her love in order to conceal my mistrust, what purpose would it serve? A moment's illusion of togetherness, an intoxication that would be over by tomorrow – and I would not even know where I stood with her on the matter of Rissen.

I began by tying a handkerchief over her mouth, so that she would not scream during the actual struggle. Of course she woke up and tried to free herself, but in addition to being much stronger than her, I had all the advantages on my side. It was not hard to keep her still while I bound her hand and foot so that she could not wriggle away. After all, I had to have both hands free.

When I stuck the needle in she jerked, but after that she did not move. She had doubtless realized that it was futile to resist.

I reckoned that it took eight minutes for the liquid to have the proper effect. When the eight minutes were up, I untied the handkerchief. By her general expression I saw that the injection had worked. She had almost regained the same girlish face she had had in her sleep.

'I know what you're doing,' she said thoughtfully, and her voice even had a tinge of the same childlike quality as her face. 'You want to know something. What do you want to know? There is too much that you ought to know. I have too much to say. I don't know where to begin. I myself want to do it, why must you force me? But perhaps I would never have been able to do it otherwise. That's how it's been all these years. There's something I want to say or do, and I don't know what it is. Perhaps there've been lots of trivial matters, friendliness and comfort and caressing, and when they were impossible the big, important things were also impossible. One single thing I know, *it* I know: that I would like to kill you. If only I knew that it would never be discovered, I would kill you. Though actually what does it matter if it's discovered, I'll do it anyway. That is better than leaving it as it is. I hate you because you can't rescue me from this, I would have killed you if I hadn't been afraid. Now I dare to do it. Only not as long as I can talk to you. I have never been able to talk to you. You are afraid, and I am afraid, and everyone is afraid. Alone, completely alone, and not pleasantly alone, as when we were young. It's dreadful. I haven't been able to talk to you about the children, about how sad I've been that Ossu has gone, and how afraid I am of the day when Maryl will be gone, and Laila. I thought you would despise me. You can despise me now, I don't care. I often wish I were a young girl again and unhappily in love instead of happily. Do you know that it's an enviable thing to be a young girl and unhappily in love, although you don't realize it at the time? When you're a young girl, you believe that there's something else, a freedom that will come with love, a kind of refuge that will exist with the person you love, a kind of warmth and a kind of rest – something that doesn't exist. Unhappily in love – one goes around in sweet despair because *I* didn't find the great happiness with *you* – and so one believes that others may have found it, and it's there, it's there to be found – and you must understand that when there is so much joy in the world and all thirst has a goal, so things are not hopeless even

if one is unhappy. Not desperate. But happily in love, it glides
out into emptiness. For there is no goal, there is only loneliness,
and why should there be anything else, why should there be a
meaning for us individuals? I have loved you too much, Leo,
and so you weren't there, either. I think I could probably kill
you now.'

'And Rissen?' I asked hoarsely, afraid that the precious minutes would trickle away before I had discovered what I wanted
to know. 'What do you think about Rissen?'

'Rissen?' she echoed, wonderingly. 'Yes, Rissen . . . There
was something special about Rissen. What was it? He wasn't
far away, like all the others. He didn't make anyone afraid, he
wasn't afraid himself.'

'Were you in love with him? Do you still love him?'

'Rissen? Was I in love with him? No – no, no. If only I could
have been. He was just not like other people. Close. Calm.
Secure. Not like you, and not like me. Had one of us been like
him – or both, both, Leo . . . But it would have been you. That's
why I want to kill you, just to get away from you, for there will
never be anyone but you, and it won't be you, either.'

She began to grow restless, and frowned. I had not dared to
take with me more Kallocain than enough for one injection, it
would have been too dangerous. And now I didn't know what
I should ask her.

'How can it be?' she whispered in anguish. 'How can it be,
that we search for something that doesn't exist? How can it be
that we are sick unto death, when we're completely well, when
all is as it should be . . .'

Her voice sank to a murmur, and by the greenish colour on
her cheeks I concluded that she was in the process of waking. I
supported the back of her head and brought the glass to her
lips. She was still tied up – had probably not noticed it under
the sedation. Now I untied her, though I wondered with some
trepidation what she would do when she was free. All the time
I had looked forward with a mixture of fear and triumph to
the moment when she would be seized with shame and remorse
at her involuntary outspokenness. I noticed that my hand was
shaking, to the point where it could not hold her head still. So

I laid her down on the pillow again and stared with fixed anxiety into the relaxed features.

But the reaction I was waiting for didn't seem to come. When she opened her eyes they were very thoughtful, but just as calmly wide open as usual, and they met my own without turning away. Her mouth frightened me. The red bow did not want to grow taut as usual, it remained passive and slack, so that her face retained its childlike expression from her sleep and the drug. I did not know that in such a lack of control there could be a solemnity that inspired fear. Her lips moved faintly, as though she were repeating her words to herself. I had nothing to say to her, could not disturb her, just sat still and looked at her face.

In the end she fell asleep, though I sat keeping watch over her. She slept, and silently I undressed and also tried to sleep, but could not. I was flooded by a deep shame and anguish. From the way I felt, one might have thought that I, not she, was the subject being examined and exposed. All along I had been clear in the perception that no matter what she might say, she would be in my power afterwards, in a different way from before. When she woke up she would have revealed secrets that ought not to be revealed, secrets that I could threaten to disclose if she took so much as a single hostile step towards me. Perhaps she already had, I didn't know. Her threat to kill me – I had heard this kind of thing many times during my work and knew that the threats were rarely carried out – but perhaps it was dangerous for her, why not? It was possible that I had her in my hand, it was possible that everything had gone according to plan.

Except for one point: I would never be able to exploit any advantage. Everything she had said was said from within myself. I was sick, unstrung to the roots of my being, because she had held herself like a mirror in front of me. I had not suspected that she, with her tight lips, with her silence and her penetrating eyes, was made of the same weak timber as I. How could I threaten her, how could I force her, when that was how it was?

After a short sleep I woke, several hours too early. Linda was asleep. The night's experiences were clear to me at the very moment I awoke, but there was also a nagging anxiety about

something that had not been done. A moment later I knew
what it was: Rissen. Today.

Now I felt like postponing the whole matter again, but could
find no justification for my inertia. Was not *that* problem at
least the same today as it had been yesterday? Rissen was certainly the same. It was not, never had been, because he might
possibly be my rival that I felt I had to get rid of him. My loath-
ing was much deeper than that. It simply felt less intrusive
today, whatever its cause. But if I did not do this now, I would
despise myself. Now, by chance, I had ample time to formulate
my police denunciation, before Linda woke up, and the night's
events had brought at least *one* good thing: I knew that she
belonged not with Rissen, but with me.

By the feeble glow of the nightlight I wrote a rough draft of my
denunciation. I had gone through it in my thoughts so often that
the basic motivation was an easy matter. Everything I had said to
Karrek in general terms I now repeated in eloquent and convincing phrases. I still had plenty of time, and sitting on the bed I
wrote the final version, none the worse for being done in foun-
tain pen with a volume of *Chemistry Journal* to lean on. I put my
name and my address firmly at the bottom, as that was required,
and on an envelope I wrote the address of police headquarters in
capital letters. I spent three-quarters of an hour reading over and
over what I had written, and brooding about my new reluctance
and hesitation. Not until the neighbours' alarm clock rang,
reminding me that the deadline would soon be here, did I draw
Karrek's secret sign in one corner, as I had already done numer-
ous times in my imagination. Then I put the document in the
envelope and stuffed the whole thing in the journal.

Linda woke up when our alarm clock also rang. We looked
at each other as though the night had been a dream. Before all
this really happened, I had imagined quite a different morning,
one on which I sat as victor and judge, dictating the victor's
demands to an exposed and broken Linda, who had to submit
to my tender mercies. But it was not to be.

We simply got up, dressed, ate in silence, took the lift
up together and parted outside the metro station. When I
turned round to see if she had gone, I noticed that she also

turned – and nodded. This brought me up short. Perhaps she still planned to lull me into a false sense of security in order to take her revenge later? But for some reason that lay on the other side of all common sense, I did not think so. When a moment later she ducked down into the jaws of the metro, I turned round and put the letter in the mailbox.

It was strange about that little sign in the corner. I knew Karrek well enough to know that it would wipe Rissen from the face of the earth. In the middle of the street, in the swarm of fellow soldiers who were hurrying to morning gymnastics and work, I suddenly stood still for a moment, struck by a terrible awareness of power. I could repeat my manoeuvre any time I liked. As long as I did not come into conflict with Karrek's own interests, he would willingly offer me dozens of lives for the service I had done him. I had power.

I have already mentioned the staircase I saw as the symbol of life. A perfectly innocent symbol, though absurd: the picture of an obedient schoolboy's progress from one form to the next, a decorous official's promotion through the grades. With a sense of revulsion I now suddenly saw myself on the topmost level. Not that I lacked the imagination to envision higher grades of power than being in favour with the chief of police in Chemistry City No. 4. Up there, I had imagination, I had material to build with, if I wished to contemplate greater heights and wider perspectives: the military rank system, the ministers in the capital – Tuareg, Lavris. But the tiny, tiny bit of power I saw before me right now was enough to be a symbol of it all. And it disgusted me.

Of course it was right, of course it was desirable that vermin like Rissen were exterminated. It wasn't that. But I struggled with doubt that it would really be possible to get very far with such a war of extermination. A few days ago it had seemed rather simple: one killed Rissen, so Rissen was gone, including the Rissen inside myself, as he had been implanted there by the other, living Rissen. One killed Rissen, and then one was a real fellow soldier again, a happy, healthy cell in the organism of the State. Since then something had happened, something that made me uncertain: the events of the night – my failure with Linda.

That it was a *failure*, I could not conceal from myself. True, I had learned what I wanted to know – that she would not stand in the way of my decision with regard to Rissen. True, deep down I was not afraid of any revenge on her part, as in the last analysis she was just as indissolubly and desperately bound to me as I to her. True, I now had her in my power, I was in possession of secrets that she did not want to be revealed. True, all of it. So if I thought in terms of the stupid, limited goal I had set for myself, it was not a failure. And yet in another, greater sense it was a basic and monstrous one.

Her words about unhappy love for which one could be envied sounded girlishly romantic, but they held a truth of a kind, one that I could very well apply to my own relationship with Linda. My marriage had in a way been an unhappy love, a reciprocated love of course, but unhappy all the same. Into a serious face, a tensed red bow-mouth, two stern, wide-open eyes, I had dreamt a secret world that would slake my thirst, soothe my anxiety, give me the ultimate security that would last forever, if only I knew of a means to enter in. And now – now by force I had penetrated as far inside as it was possible to go, forced my way to what she did not want to give me, and yet my thirst was still there, my anxiety and my insecurity greater than ever. If there was a counterpart to my dream world, it was inaccessible to all my efforts. And like Linda, I was ready to wish my way back to my enviable illusion, where I still believed that the paradise behind the wall could be gained.

I found it hard to explain what this had to do with my revulsion at power, but I sensed that there was a connection. I sensed that even if Rissen were killed it would prove to be no more than a drop in the ocean. Just as I had attained what I set out to do with Linda, discovered what I wanted to know and yet failed so profoundly that without exaggeration I could speak of despair, so also I could attain what I had set myself with regard to Rissen – a judgement, an execution – and yet not move one inch further towards what I was really striving for. For the first time in my life I sensed what power was, felt it in my hand like a weapon – and despaired.

CHAPTER 16

A whisper passed through police headquarters. No one knew anything, no one had said anything definite, but everyone had heard it like a low breathing when they met on stairways and in corridors when no witnesses were within earshot: 'The police minister himself – Tuareg – have you heard – just a rumour – arrested for treasonous thinking – sssh . . .'

What was Karrek's view of this, I wondered to myself – when he had been so eager to have the new law passed? Did he know about it? Perhaps it was actually him . . . ?

Of course I had nothing to do with the rumour; I plunged back into my work.

At the lunch table I no longer avoided meeting Rissen's gaze. If he could see through me now it would in any case be too late for him to ward off the blow. In addition, I had a peculiar feeling that he was not quite real. What sat there at the table blowing its nose in its handkerchief quite tangibly and audibly, was a kind of mirage, a relatively harmless mirror-image of an evil principle I wanted to bring to life. I had aimed my blow, and in a moment the blow would strike – the mirror image. Yet I tried to persuade myself that it was exactly the same thing . . .

Not until I was on my way home did the soporific feeling of being in a dream let go. When I thought about how I must see Linda again, my feet became heavy. I had a night off ahead of me, and very soon we would be alone with each other, the two of us, eyeball to eyeball. I did not know how I would get through it.

So then the moment came. She must have been waiting for it. Today it was she who drew up the chairs, and she who turned on the radio – but neither of us heard the programme, just as little now as previously.

For a long time we sat in silence. I stole a quick look at her face – it seemed to be working in there, behind the immobility. But she said nothing. What if I were mistaken – what if my qualms of that morning were justified?

'Have you denounced me?' I asked in a thick voice.

She shook her head.

'But you're planning to?'

'No, Leo, no, no.'

Then she was silent again, and there was no question that I could ask. I did not know how I was going to endure it. At last I closed my eyes and leaned back in my chair, submitting to something unknown but unavoidable. I had a sudden memory of a young man we had had under injection, the one who had talked about the secret meetings of the sect of fools. He had said something about the terrible effect of silence, about how helplessly naked a silent person is, and right now I understood him.

'I want to talk with you,' she said finally, with effort. 'For a long time. You must listen. Will you?'

'Yes,' I said. 'Linda, I have done you harm.'

She smiled a small, quivering smile.

'You have broken me open like a tin can, by force,' she said. 'But it's not enough. Afterwards I realized that either I must die of shame, or I must go on voluntarily. May I go on? Do you want a little more of me, Leo?'

I could not answer, and from that moment on I cannot account for what happened within me, as not the slightest part of me did anything but listen. I have the distinct notion that until that moment I had never listened in all my life. What I had earlier called listening was in its very essence different from this. Then my ears had done their job in their place, my thoughts in theirs, my memory had registered everything in exemplary fashion, while my interest lay somewhere else, I don't know where. Now: I knew nothing except what she told me, I disappeared in it, *was* her.

'You already know something about me, Leo. You know that I have dreamt of killing you. Last night, when all my shame and fear were gone, I thought I would be able to do it, but now I know that I can't. I can only dream desperate dreams. And yet I don't think it's the fear of punishment that stops me. Perhaps I'll be able to explain it later. It's something else that I want to talk to you about now. I want to talk about the children, and what – what I've learned about the children. It will take a long time. I've never dared to say anything about it. I shall start from the beginning, with Ossu.

'Do you remember when I was carrying Ossu? Do you remember that we were always certain it must be a boy? I don't know, perhaps you just went along with my wishful imaginings, but at least you said you also thought it would be a boy. You know, I think I would have been dreadfully insulted if it had been a girl – I would have taken it as an injustice to myself, I, who was such a loyal fellow soldier that I would gladly have died if a means had been discovered to make women superfluous. Yes, for I saw them as a necessary evil – necessary for the time being. Of course I was aware that officially we were considered to be just as valuable or nearly as valuable as men – but only at second hand, only because we were able to give birth to more men, and more women, too, of course, who in their turn could give birth to more men. And no matter how much it hurt my vanity – after all, one wants so much to have a tiny little value, no, that isn't true, one wants to have a great big value – no matter how much it hurt, I had no trouble admitting that I *wasn't* worth very much. Women *aren't* as good as men, I told myself, they don't have as much physical strength, can't lift such heavy objects, don't bear up so well in air raids, their nerves are not as sturdy on a battlefield, they are on the whole worse warriors, worse fellow soldiers than men. Their officially being granted equal status is a courtesy, everyone knows that it's a courtesy, to make them happy and complaisant. There may perhaps come a time, I thought, when it turns out that women are superfluous, when it will be possible to utilize their ovaries and throw the rest down the drain. Then the whole State can be filled with men, and need not go to the wasteful expense of providing girls with nourishment and education. Of course it gave you a strangely empty feeling sometimes to know that you were only a depository, necessary in the short term, but far too expensive. Well, but since I was honest enough to admit it – would it really have been *such* a great disappointment if the first time I gave birth I produced something that was also just a depository? But it didn't turn out like that, Ossu was luckily a man in the making, and I had almost acquired a purpose. That's how loyal I was in those days, Leo.

'Yes, so I saw him grow and begin to walk, and meanwhile I was carrying Maryl. Since I'd more or less finished nursing Ossu, I only saw him in the mornings and evenings, before I went to my job in the morning and when I came home at night – but it was so strange. I knew, with all my conviction, that he belonged to the State, that he was already being trained in the creche all day as a future fellow soldier and that the same training would continue in the children's camp and the youth camp. Apart from the genetic material, which of course I knew was important – and in our case perfectly in order, as far as it could be verified – and which incidentally isn't "our" property, either, as it's inherited from other fellow soldiers before us – I felt absolutely certain that his future character depended on his superiors at the creche, at the children's camp, at the youth camp, on their own example and on the rules they followed in his training. But I couldn't help noticing a number of comical traits which I recognized as coming from you and from myself. I noticed his way of wrinkling his nose, and I thought: "That's so funny, I used to do that when I was little!" In that way, I came back, in my son. It was a proud feeling: in him I was almost growing up to be a man! And I noticed his laugh, which reminds me so much of yours. In that way I almost managed to be present at your childhood. And his way of twisting his head, you know, and something about the shape of his eyes ... There wasn't anything odd about it, but it gave me a criminal sense of ownership. "You can see that he's ours," I thought – "our son", I added guiltily, as I knew that this wasn't a loyal feeling. No, it certainly was not, but it was there. The worst thing was that it was getting stronger, and strongest of all in connection with the little unborn child I was carrying ... Perhaps you remember that Maryl's birth was complicated and took a long time? It's probably superstition, but even back then I imagined, and I couldn't get rid of the thought, that it was because I was so reluctant to let her go. When Ossu was born I was still a mother entirely in the spirit of the State, a mother who only gave birth for the State. When Maryl was born I was a selfish, grasping female creature, one that only gave birth for herself and thought she had a right to what she gave birth to. My conscience told me that I was in the wrong, that such thoughts were impermissible, but no feelings of guilt and shame could drive away the greed that had woken in me. If I have any possessive tendencies – they're not very strong, Leo, you must admit! – but they're there – they emerged during the time after Maryl was born. During the brief hours when Ossu was at home I bossed him around, dominated him as much as I could, just so as to feel that he was still mine. And he obeyed – for if one learns any-thing at the creche, it's above all to obey orders, and I knew that for the time being, at least, I still had a right to that, it was part of the State's will and the training of fellow soldiers. But those were just excuses. My way of treating Ossu wasn't *really* a token of regard for the State. It was an attempt to get as much of a sense of possession as I could in the short time I still had him at home.

'When Maryl was born, I was surprised at how calmly I took it that she was a girl, perhaps not just calmly, actually: I was even pleased. She didn't belong primarily to the State as much as a boy would have, she was more mine – she was more me, as she was a girl.

'How can I describe what happened to me after that? You know, Maryl is a strange child. She was neither you nor I. It's possible that some ancestors on her father's or mother's side have reappeared in her character – but I didn't know who they were, and it was all so far in the past. She was just Maryl. It sounds so simple, but it was so strange. She must have seen things in her own way even then, even before she could speak. And later – yes, you know. You know that she's a law unto herself.

'I noticed that my greedy grasp had loosened. Maryl wasn't mine. For long periods of time I would sit and listen to her singing to herself, or reading, what should I call them? – imaginative dream stories, which she had never learned at the creche. So where had she got them? Dream tales can't be part of your genetic material and pop up in your family tree! She had a melody of her own, and she didn't get it from us or from the creche. Do you understand that the thought made me light-headed? She was Maryl. She wasn't like anyone else. She wasn't a shapeless lump of clay that you or I or the State simply had to mould after some random pattern. Not my property or creation. I was fascinated by my own child, in a new, shy, unfamiliar way. When she was close to me, I was silent and apprehensive. It dawned on me that Ossu was also probably a law unto himself, though by now he had got far enough to know how to conceal himself. I regretted having been so greedy about him, and I finally left him in peace. Those days were full of wonder and excitement and life.

'Then I discovered that there was another child on the way. Nothing could have been more natural – but for me it was overwhelming. That I was afraid is not the right word. I wasn't afraid that something would happen to me, wasn't afraid of giving birth or anything like that. I was horrified because I thought that for the first time I could discern the unfathomable. It would be my third child, and yet I thought that never until then had I known what it was to give birth. It no longer struck me that I was a production machine that was too expensive. Nor was I a greedy owner. What was I, then? I don't know. Someone who had no control over what happened – and yet exalted almost to the point of ecstasy because it had to happen through me. Inside me a being was coming into existence – and it already had features – it already had its own character – and I couldn't change it ... I was a branch that blossomed and I knew nothing of my roots or trunk, but I could feel the sap rising from unknown depths ...

'I've had to talk for a long time, and yet I don't know if you understand me. I mean: if you understand that it's something beneath and behind us. That it's created in us. I know that I shouldn't say this, for it's only the State that owns us. But I'm saying it to you anyway. Otherwise everything is meaningless.'

She fell silent, and I sat speechless, though I felt like scream-ing. Here is everything I have fought against, I thought as in a dream. Everything I have fought against and been afraid of and yearned for.

She knew nothing of the fools and their desert city, and yet she would fall under the law just as inexorably as they, because she dreamed of a connection that was other than that of the State. What was more: I would fall under it too. Did I not already know that other connection, lawless and ineluctable, between her and me?

I was trembling from head to foot. I wanted to say: yes, yes! It would have brought relief, as when someone completely exhausted is able to fall asleep. I was freed from a connection that was choking me, and rescued for something new, self-evident and simple, something that bore me along but did not bind me.

My lips wrestled with words that did not exist and could not be said. I wanted to go, I wanted to act, I wanted to break everything and make everything new. There was no world for me any more, no place to dwell in. Nothing but the firm con-nection between Linda and me.

I went over to her, knelt down on the floor and put my head in her lap.

I don't know if anyone has done such a thing before or if anyone will do it again. I have never heard of it. I only know that I was compelled, and that it contained all that I wanted to say and could not.

She must have understood. She put her hand on my head. We remained in that position for a long, long time.

CHAPTER 17

Late at night I sprang up and said:

'I must save Rissen. I've denounced Rissen.'

She asked no questions. I rushed upstairs to the concierge, woke him and asked if I could use the internal phone. When he heard that I wanted to talk to the police chief, he made no objections.

Karrek could not be reached, he had given strict instructions that no one was to disturb him at night. After much bustle and to-ing and fro-ing, a sensible guard came to the phone and calmed me, saying that, after all, no matter could be settled in the middle of the night. On the other hand, if I wanted to meet the police chief an hour before work began early tomorrow morning, he would at any rate inform him, and I could present myself on time and find out if he would receive me.

I went back to Linda.

Still she asked no questions. I don't know if it was because she understood everything or because she was waiting for me to say something. But I could not speak, not yet. My tongue had always been an agile and reliable tool, but now it refused to serve me. Just as I had recently listened for the first time in my life, I knew that if I wanted to speak now, it must be in a new way for which I was not yet ready. After all, those layers of myself that were now to make themselves heard had never before formed any words. Nor did they need to, yet. I had said what I had to say – and Linda had understood me – when I put my head on her knee.

We were silent again, but it was a silence of a different kind than the one that had tormented me earlier. Now we were just waiting patiently together, and we were over the hardest part of it.

At night, when neither of us could get to sleep, Linda said:

'Do you think there are more people who have experienced this? Perhaps among your test subjects. I must find them.'

I thought of the transparent little woman whom I had shocked out of her false self-confidence with such a sweet sense of envy. What bitter stage of mistrust had she reached now? I thought of the sect of fools, who pretended to be asleep among people who were armed. They must all be in prison by now.

Later she said:

'Do you think there are more people who have experienced this – others? Who have begun to understand what it means to give birth? Other mothers? Or fathers? Or lovers? Who haven't dared to say what they have seen, but will dare to if others do. I must find them.'

I thought of the woman with the deep voice, the one who had talked about the organic and the organized. If she had avoided prison, I still did not know where she was.

And later, from far away, as from an ocean of sleep:

'Perhaps a new world may grow from those who are mothers – whether they are men or women, and whether they have given birth to children or not. But where are they?'

Then I jumped up and was wide awake and thought of Rissen, who all the time had known what was in me and had probed and searched for it, until I abandoned him to death. I groaned aloud and pressed myself violently to Linda.

CHAPTER 18

An hour before work began, I presented myself at police head-quarters. Karrek received me.

I realized what a genuine service he was doing me by getting up so early to receive me, without knowing the nature of my errand, what was more. He probably expected something quite different from what I was bringing him, the exposure of some enormous nest of spies or something of that sort.

'I – I put that sign on the . . .' I began, stammering.

'I know nothing of any signs,' he said, coldly and blandly. 'What do you mean, Fellow Soldier Kall?'

I realized he considered that there were witnesses to his words. A police headquarters, too, there are wires in the walls, ears and eyes to reckon with, and there are probably circumstances where even the chief of police must watch out for himself. I thought of the whispering rumour about Tuareg.

'I did something wrong,' I said (as if that could be of any help now!). I mean – I mean: I sent in a denunciation. I just want to – ask if I can withdraw it.'

With an air of the most extreme complaisance, Karrek made telephone calls and had a package of documents brought in so that he could search for my denunciation. He made me wait for a long time, before looking up with a glint in his eye.

'Impossible,' he said. 'Even if the suspect had not already been arrested – and he has – the police could naturally not ignore such an extraordinarily well-motivated accusation. Your request is denied.'

I stared him in the face, but its charged immobility held no expression. Either he was under surveillance, and then he would not dare to show any compliance with my requests, especially not after my foolish words of introduction. Or else – I was now in disfavour. What use did Karrek have for a henchman who failed?

Whatever the truth of the matter, right now it was impossible to speak frankly with the police chief.

'In that case,' I said, 'I can only ask – that – that – he isn't condemned to death, at least.'

'Such matters do not lie within my jurisdiction at all,' said Karrek, coldly. 'His sentence depends completely upon the judge. Actually, I can inform you that his case has already been allocated to a certain judge, but I don't consider it within my rights to tell you his name, as it would clearly be a criminal act to try to influence a judge *ex ante.*'

I felt my legs give under me and had to grip the desk in order not to fall. Karrek did not notice, or pretended not to. In my distress I thought: If he is under surveillance and doesn't dare to show that we are old friends then perhaps he will help me later, in secret. All this is just game-playing. For I've always been able to pin my hopes on him before.

I straightened up, saw Karrek smile sardonically, and heard him say with honey-soft politeness:

'It may perhaps interest you to know that it is you who will administer the Kallocain injection in the case of Edo Rissen. You are next in line, as the regular injector is presently himself being injected. One of the students could have been assigned to the task, but it was thought that you should be given the honour.'

Only later did I begin to suspect that this was not true, that not until that moment had Karrek felt like compelling me to take part, either to restore me to reason and energy by such drastic means – or simply to torment me.

At any rate, it all went as he had said. After the lunch break I was called to the judicial proceedings in the Edo Rissen case, and I had to keep my students busy as best I could. My morning had been so chaotic that several times I nearly cancelled and excused myself on grounds of illness. That in spite of it all I managed to continue was due to the fact that I had to, that I *wanted* to be present at Rissen's trial and sentencing, less in order to influence the course of events – something I did not think possible – than to once again see and hear the man of whom I had been so afraid and whom I believed that I hated so deeply.

In the courtroom a large crowd had already gathered. I picked out the tall military figure who served as judge, and the two secretaries, who sat staring at their empty writing pads. At the judge's side sat people in military and police uniform – presumably specialist advisers in various fields, psychologists, State ethics consultants, economists and others – and in front of all these, in a rising semi-circle, sat the students, Rissen's own students, in work uniform. At first I saw their faces like skin-coloured misty blotches in the mass of uniforms. Then it occurred to me to watch how they reacted. With effort I fixed my attention on a few faces, one after the other, but they seemed like masks. I released them, and they floated out into mist as before. At the same moment the door opened and Rissen was led in, handcuffed.

He looked round the courtroom without focusing on anyone in particular, and not on me, either. And why would he have focused on me? He could know neither that I had informed on him nor that I was devouring all his movements and expressions in hungry desperation. A glimmer of hope passed through me: perhaps not I alone – perhaps more than I sat here with the same hungry desperation behind the mask? Perhaps many?

When he had settled himself in his chair, in an unassuming, non-military manner as was his habit – sometimes he almost seemed to disappear amid his sturdy physicality, perhaps because he did not force himself on one any more than objects and trees and animals do – he closed his eyes and smiled. It was a helpless and slightly weary smile that made no demands on anyone – as if all the time he perceived his absolute solitude and existed in it; even sought peace and quiet in it, in the way I can imagine a sleepy polar explorer seeks peace and quiet in the cold, even though he knows it may send him to sleep forever. And while the Kallocain was working, this helpless smile spread like a peaceful blessing over his furrowed face. Even if hours

passed before he spoke, you couldn't take your eyes off him.
Where had I been looking before, never to have noticed what a
peculiar dignity there was in this polite and gently disengaged
man, whom I had always found ridiculous? A dignity that was
quite separate from the stiff dignity of the military type, because
it consisted in a complete indifference to how he seemed to
others. When he opened his eyes and began to talk, one had the
impression that he might just as well have been sitting back in
any chair at all, staring up at the white lights in the ceiling and
talking without a drop of Kallocain in him, talking in the same
way as now, because the fear and the shame that held us others
back, in him had been eaten away by loneliness and lack of
hope. I myself could have gone up to him and asked him to
speak, and perhaps he would have done so, voluntarily, like
Linda, only as a gift. He would have said everything about
what I wanted to hear, about the fools and their secret tradition, about the desert city, and about himself, how he in his
way had been forced out into the unknown just as Linda had in
hers – everything, had I not chosen to play the enemy in my
wild terror, when I noticed that something forbidden in me
responded to his tone with the same resonance and would never
let itself be silenced again. He would have talked for longer
than one could make him talk now, and made me aware of real-
ities in myself that now I would never discover. I had no
overwhelming sympathy with him because he was going to be
sentenced and die, but I was wild with bitterness at having
mutilated myself by informing on him. And I listened as devour-
ingly as I had listened to Linda, only with greater anguish.

I had wanted to know something about him. But he did not
talk about anything personal. General topics filled him to the
point of bursting.

'Just so,' he said, 'just so. Here I am, then. As it must be. A
question of time. If truth be told. Can you hear the truth? Not
everyone is true enough to hear the truth, that is the sad thing.
It could be a bridge between one person and another – as long
as it is voluntary, yes – as long as it given like a gift and received
like a gift. Isn't it strange that everything loses its value as soon
as it ceases to be a gift – even the truth? No, you haven't noticed

it, of course, because then you would see that you've been scraped bare, exposed right down to your naked skeleton – and who has the strength to see that? Who wants to see his wretchedness until he is compelled to? Not compelled by human beings. Compelled by the emptiness and the cold – the Arctic cold that threatens all of us. Community, you say – community? Welded together? And that is what you shout, each from your own side of an abyss. Was there no point, not one, not one, in the long evolution of the race, when another path could have been chosen? Must the path go over the abyss? No point where the armoured chariot of Power could have been stopped from rolling towards the emptiness? Is there a way through death to new life? Is there a holy place where fate turns around?

'I have brooded for years about where that place may be. Will we be there when we have devoured the neighbour state, or the neighbour state devours us? Will roads grow between people as easily as they are growing between cities and districts? Let it come soon, then. Let it come, let it come, with all its horrors! Or will that not help, either? Will the armoured chariot have grown so powerful by then that it can no longer be transformed from a god into a tool? Can a god, even though he is the most dead of all gods, relinquish his power voluntarily? – I would so much like to believe that there was a green depth in man, an ocean of intact growing power that would melt all the dead remnants in its mighty crucible, healing and creating for eternity . . . But I haven't seen it. What I know is that sick parents and sick teachers are producing children who are even sicker, until sickness has become the norm and health a bogeyman. Lonely people give birth to those who are even lonelier, frightened people to those who are even more frightened . . . Where may a single remnant of health have hidden itself to grow and break through the armour? . . . Those poor people we called fools played with their symbols. There was still something – they at least knew that there was something they lacked. As long as they knew what they were doing there was still something left. But it doesn't lead anywhere! Where can anything lead? If I went and stood outside a metro station when the crowds were surging up at their densest, or at a big celebration with loudspeakers in front of me – my cries would still not penetrate further than to one or two eardrums in the million-mile World State, and from there they would bounce back as empty sound. I'm a cog. I'm a creature from which they have taken the life . . . And yet: right now I know that it isn't true. It's the Kallocain that's making me full of irrational hope, of course – everything is becoming light and clear and calm. At least I'm alive – in spite of all they have taken from me – and right now I know that *what I am is on the way somewhere.* I have seen death's power spread out across the world in wider and wider circles – but must not life's power also have its circles, even though I haven't been able to see them? . . . Yes, yes, I know that it's the effect of the Kallocain, but can't it be true, even so?'

On the way to the courtroom wild fantasies had whirled around in my brain – how for some odd reason all the listeners simultaneously looked elsewhere and I was able to whisper my questions in Rissen's ear . . . Even then I knew it was a day-dream that could not be fulfilled, and of course in reality not one of the listeners, let alone all of them at once, turned their attentive gaze away from Rissen. But strangely enough: even had I had a chance to do so, I would have had nothing to ask. What now did I care about the desert city, what did I care about the fools' traditions? No desert city was as inaccessible and safe as the one I was headed for, and it lay not miles away somewhere unknown, but near, near. Linda would still be there. She at least would still be there.

Rissen gave a sigh and closed his eyes, but opened them again.

'They know!' he murmured, and his smile grew brighter and less helpless. 'They're afraid, they're taking a stand – so they know. My wife knows, when she won't listen and tells me to be quiet. The students know, when they put on their most super-cilious expressions and mock me. It may have been one of them who informed on me, my wife or one of the students. Whoever did it – *knew.* When I speak, they hear themselves. When I'm active and am present, it's themselves they're afraid of. Oh, if

only it existed, that green depth, that indestructible place –
and now I believe it exists. It's probably the Kallocain, but I'm
glad all the same . . . that I . . . can believe it . . .'

'My chief,' I said to the judge in a voice that I tried in vain to
keep steady, 'shall I give him another injection? He is already
waking up.'

But the judge shook his head.

'That's enough,' he said. 'The case is already sufficiently
clear. Don't you think so, advisers? Don't you agree with me
on this case?'

The advisers murmured their agreement and withdrew in
order to deliberate with the judge. Just as they were opening
the door to the adjacent room, something unexpected happened. A young man from Rissen's course jumped up from his
place in the middle of the rising semi-circle, rushed down to
the podium, where I was in the process of relieving the subject's nausea on waking up, and signalled wildly to those who
were leaving in an effort to make them stay.

'I'm the man who caused all this!' he shouted desperately. 'It
was I who denounced my chief Edo Rissen for treasonous thinking! This morning on my way to work I put my denunciation in
the mailbox; when I got there he'd already been arrested! But
everyone here who heard him . . . must realize . . .'

I stepped down from the podium, went over to the young
man and put my hand on his mouth.

'Calm down,' I whispered, 'you will gain nothing, you will
just make yourself unhappy and you won't rescue anyone.
Others have also denounced him.'

Aloud I said:

'Such disorderly scenes by people who have lost their sense
of balance will absolutely not be permitted while the inquiry is
in progress. You, Fellow Soldier, there in the first row, will you
please pour a glass of water and hand it over here. One must
understand and excuse the confusion in a loyal young man
when he is forced to denounce his superior – but calm down,
calm down, you really don't need to take it so hard. You really
don't need to stand and defend yourself in public. You are perfectly within your rights as it is.'

In confusion he drank the water and stared at me. When he looked as though he wanted to say more, I firmly silenced him and promised to speak to him at the end of the inquiry. He sat down at the very end of the first row and closed his eyes.

When I jumped up on the podium again, Rissen was wide awake. He sat still, looking straight out into space, and still smiling to himself in his loneliness, though now the smile was a bitter one. Suddenly he staggered up from his chair and took a few steps towards the auditorium. I was neither able nor willing to stop him.

'You that have heard me . . .' he began in a voice that penetrated to the furthest corner, and yet he did not shout, but spoke dark and low. To the day I die I will hear the resonance and intensity of his dark, low voice. Two policemen who all this time had been waiting in the background rushed out, placed a gag on his mouth and led him back to his chair. The courtroom was deathly still as at last the judge, followed by his advisers, trooped up on the podium at a steady, measured pace and settled down to pronounce the judgement. The whole courtroom rose. Rissen, too, was raised to attention by the two policemen.

'A bacillus-carrier can be disinfected,' said the judge, in a tone of solemn command. 'But an individual who by his very bearing, by his very breathing spreads such discontent with all our institutions, mistrust about the future, defeatism on the question of the neighbour state's attempts to conduct brigandage on our borderlands, he can never be disinfected. He is harmful to the State wherever and in whatever work he undertakes and can only be rendered harmless by death. This judgement I pronounce in unanimity with the best of the advice I have received from the experts appointed to the case. Edo Rissen is condemned to death.'

A solemn hush greeted the judgement. The young man, my co-informer, sat rigid in his chair, white as a sheet. Rissen, still gagged, was led outside. When the door closed after him, I was standing right next to it. Without being aware of it, I had followed him step by step, as far as I could go.

When I looked round, the young man had gone. As he was

one of the students on the course, it would be easy to track him down. My thoughts dwelt mechanically on a few everyday questions: who would now teach Rissen's course, probably one of the more advanced students, who would teach my course if I had to take over Rissen's, yes, there were so many people to choose from, though actually we could not afford to do without a single one of them, soon this course would be finally over, so then we could begin another . . . It was the rattling of a mill grinding emptiness. I myself was somewhere where it was still and dark.

When I returned to my own lecture room and stood before a listening semi-circle, confusingly like the one I had just left, if you ignored the judge and his advisers, I finally had to excuse myself on the grounds of feeling unwell, and go home. I could not continue this play-acting any more.

I went into the parents' room, shut the door behind me, unfolded the bed and threw myself on it in a kind of semi-stupor. The nightlight was on, the fan was humming; outside I heard the home help moving about at her chores. I heard the door slam shut when she went to fetch the children. Then Maryl's and Laila's voices and noise and the home help's attempts to make them be quiet. I heard the creaking of the dumb waiter and the clatter as the plates were set. But I did not hear Linda's voice, the only thing I was waiting for.

A knocking at the door made me start, and the home help asked through the crack:

'Would you like something to eat, my chief?'

I smoothed my hair and went out. But Linda was not there. It was already long past our normal dinner time. In vain I scoured my memory for whatever it was she must be doing – she always at least came home and had dinner first – but it would not do for me to show any uncertainty on Linda's account in front of the home help.

'Oh, yes of course,' I said hesitantly, 'I remember now, she said she was going to be out . . . Careless of me, I've completely forgotten what it was.'

The children were packed off to bed, and I continued to wait. The home help left, but Linda had still not arrived. In my anxiety I phoned the Accident Centre, not caring what the concierge would think. During the day a number of accidents had of course occurred in Chemistry City No. 4, a few of them on metro lines I didn't know, and some faulty ventilator systems with two deaths and a couple of uncertain cases, but none of them in the district where Linda worked.

The worst thing was that I could not sit waiting any longer. My regiment was holding a celebration that evening, and I could not be absent from it without good reason. I had been unable to do my work, but to sit and let speeches and lectures and drum-rolls pass through my ears that I would surely manage. If only I knew where Linda was.

She had talked about seeking out people. She wanted to find others who had also attained that self-evident sense of belonging. But did she know where they were? Where had she begun her search?

When it was time, I went – quite mechanically, without it occurring to me that I could play truant.

I would never see Linda again.

CHAPTER 19

It had been my intention to listen to the lecture, but that did not go well. Time after time I braced inwardly in order to pull myself together, and time after time I managed to follow a few sentences. All I remember is that it was about the development of life in the State from the most primitive division, when individuals, each a solitary centre in themselves, lived in constant insecurity – insecurity in relation to the powers of nature and insecurity in relation to other similar solitary centres – and to the finished State, which was the individual's only meaning and justification, granting complete and utter security. Such was the general gist, but I would not be able to reproduce the precise details were my life to depend on it. No sooner had I once again forced myself to pay attention than my thoughts of Linda and Rissen and the new world that existed and wanted to emerge made me forget everything around me. When I awoke from my reflections I could hardly keep still. Not only my inner self, but even my muscles and sinews were screaming for release. If I could not immediately set myself in motion, I would explode with my own energies at any moment – that was how it felt.

At last, in the middle of the lecture, I approached the exit. The police secretary on the nearest corner platform raised his eyebrows disapprovingly, and the doorman stopped me with a questioning look. I gave my name and showed my surface permit as proof of identity.

'I'm sorry, Fellow Soldier, but I don't feel well,' I said. 'I think I'll feel better if I can get up into the fresh air for a couple of minutes. I'm ill, have been in bed all day, had to be away from my job . . .'

He wrote down my name, made a note of the time I left, and then let me out.

I took the lift up. At the doorman's desk I repeated my request and here too, my name was noted and I was let out.

I stepped out on to the roof terrace.

At first I could not tell what it was that was different. From the deserted terrace something absolutely unfamiliar greeted me. I was deeply shocked, without knowing why. After a few seconds I realized what had scared me. The sound of aeroplanes, which usually filled the air night and day, was gone. There was silence.

Inside the living quarters and deep down in the laboratories I had experienced a relative silence, where the rumbling that came from the metro network and from the air was muffled by walls and earth strata and where the fans produced a faint, soporific hum; a blunting of all sounds, always a relief and a source of rest, as when sleep encloses one in its mussel shell, and one feels lonely, small and hunched up. The silence on the roof terrace was not like that relative silence. It was limitless.

On night marches and on the way home from lectures and banquets I had on countless occasions seen the stars shine forth between the mobile silhouettes of the aeroplanes, and what more could one say about it? They did not shine brightly enough to make my hooded flashlight superfluous. I had once heard that they were suns, far away, but I cannot recall that the explanation made any particular impression on me. In the boundless silence I now suddenly saw the universe stretching from infinity to infinity, and felt dizzy as I gazed at the enormous void between star and star. An overarching nothingness took my breath away.

Then I heard something I had felt and seen the effects of, but had never heard before: the wind. A gentle nocturnal breeze that crept between the walls and set the oleanders on the roof terrace in gentle motion. And although it probably only filled a few districts with its wonderful murmur, I could not with all my will ward off an overpowering sense that it was the breathing of the whole night sky, that it was growing out of the darkness gently and naturally, as when a child gives a sigh in its sleep. The night was breathing, the night was alive, and as far out in the infinite as I could see the stars were pulsating like hearts and filling the void with wave upon wave of vibrating life.

When I woke to awareness of myself again, I was sitting on the wall around the roof terrace and shivering, not with cold, as it was a warm, almost hot night, but with powerful emotion. The wind was still blowing, though more faintly, and I knew that it was born not from the darkness of space but from atmospheric layers near the earth. The stars still twinkled as brightly, and I reminded myself that their pulse-beats of light were an optical illusion. But it didn't matter. What I saw and heard might be mirages; yet they had only lent form to another universe, a universe from within – where I was used to encountering a dry, shrivelled shell that I called myself. I felt that I had touched the living depths that Rissen had cried out for and Linda had known and seen. 'Don't you know that this is where life springs up?' the woman had said in my dream. I believed her, and was certain that *anything at all could happen*.

I did not want to go back to the banquet and the lecture. Now I did not care if anyone noticed my absence. All the swarming activity that was now taking place in a thousand banquet and lecture halls underground in Chemistry City No. 4 seemed remote and unreal. I did not belong there. I was taking part in the creation of a new world.

I wanted to go home, to Linda. And what if she was not there, what if I did not meet her? Then I would carry on, go to the young man who had also informed on Rissen, go to Rissen's wife ... Where the young man lived I did not know, but I had the address of Rissen's apartment; it was in the laboratory district, where I had a permit and could come and go as I pleased. He had said: 'My wife suspects – my wife may have informed on me.' If she had put up as desperate a resistance as I had, then she was also close to understanding. First I would go home, and then to her. There was no hesitation in me any more. I was taking part in the creation of a new world.

No one was visible. As inconspicuously as I could, I slipped over the low wall that separated the roof terrace from the street.

My footsteps echoed strangely in the silence, but it did not occur to me that I might attract any attention, nor did anyone stop me. As there were no aeroplanes in the way, the stars gave enough light for me to be able to see as I went along, and I did not bother to use my flashlight. Although I had been walking completely alone up there above ground, down here under the stars I had a peculiar sensation of not being on my own. Just as I was on my way to strangers to seek the world's deep living connection, so perhaps Linda was on her way somewhere, to people I did not know. And was it not possible that right now others in the thousand cities of the World State were on their way like us, or had perhaps already got there? Only a few days ago such a thought would have made me shrink, but how can one stop short at a state border, even one that is thousands of miles long, when one has sensed that one's pulse is driven by hearts in the universe?

In the distance I could hear the district sentry's rhythmical marching, with the short pause and a short scraping each time he made a full turn. It was odd to hear such sounds out in the open air. What was the sentry, in his solitude, thinking about the silent night? Yes – what was I myself thinking? Only now did I have time to wonder where all this silence was coming from.

But only for a moment. I was unable to solve the riddle, and I did not care. The only thing that mattered was the mission I was on.

Just then a distant whirring arose and began to grow into the rumble of engines. The aeroplanes were there again. Whether it was the previous silence that made the noise so overwhelming or whether it had really not been so loud before, I could not say. Whatever the truth of it, the noise was so ear-splitting that I had to lean against the wall while my eardrums got used to it.

The air was suddenly dark all over, thick and dark, but in the darkness there was a swarming of a kind I did not recognize. Very close to me, I could feel rather than see solid bodies filling the air around me. I took out my flashlight and shone it straight ahead of me. It showed a human figure half a metre away. Paratroopers! A second later at least ten more powerful flashlights shone in my face, and I felt my arms being seized by strong hands.

Since I could only suppose that the air force was holding a night exercise, I shouted as loudly as I could, to drown out the noise:

'I'm ill, I'm on my way to the metro station! Let me go, Fellow Soldiers!'

Perhaps they could not hear me or they had different orders – but either way they did not let me go. After they had searched me and disarmed me – I was in police and military uniform because of the banquet – I was bound tightly and loaded on to a sort of narrow three-wheeled vehicle which some men had quickly assembled from lightweight components and which seemed to be especially designed for transporting prisoners. Then I was tied to the back seat, not really uncomfortably, but making it impossible for me to move, while one of the soldiers jumped into the front seat and drove the vehicle off.

I assumed that I had involuntarily ended up as a dummy prisoner in the air force's exercises and realized that all I had to do was play for time. In some way, sooner or later, I would reach where I wanted to be.

Everywhere as we rolled along, our headlamp threw a quick beam of light over a short stretch of road. A quarter of an hour ago not a soul had been heard or seen. Now all the streets, squares and roof terraces were teeming with people, each person eagerly intent on some particular task. I could not but admire the organization in this gigantic night exercise. And the further we travelled, the further the work had progressed. I saw barbed-wire barricades go up (would they really have time to clear them away before early morning, when people would need to get through in order to go to work?). I saw hosepipes being unrolled, containers of various kinds taken in different directions, guards patrolling every metro station and every residential area. Now and then I saw a three-wheeler like ours with a prisoner like myself in the back, and wondered where they were taking us.

On the square in front of a tent construction that had been

erected on a roof terrace the three-wheelers seemed to be gathering in a flock. The prisoners who had been taken there – about twenty before me – had their feet untied, but not their hands, and were swept into the tent. Just inside the doorway I collided with another prisoner, who was digging in his heels and complaining loudly over and over again that he, a district sentry, was being subjected to a dummy manoeuvre of this kind. Who was taking care of his duties in the meantime? How would he be able to explain his absence tomorrow in front of his superior? As soon as you got inside the walls of the tent the noise from the engines was much fainter – the tent was equipped with a powerful soundproofing device – so that now you could hear very clearly what the man said, and I thought the soldiers around him could at least have offered him the decency of a reply; until I suddenly heard two other soldiers exchange a few words in a totally foreign language of which I understood not a word. We were not victims of a night-training exercise. We were prisoners of the enemy.

Even today I have no idea how the whole thing had happened. It may be supposed that the enemy had slowly and methodically infiltrated the air force with spies until it eventually had every plane under its command. A wildfire of mutiny and treason, for some reason that I do not know, is another explanation that might perhaps be imagined. The possibilities are many, all equally fantastic, and all I know for certain is that there was no aerial battle, and I saw no conflict on the ground either. It must have been a well-executed surprise.

The prisoners waited in line in an outer section of the tented construction and were then admitted to an inner cell one by one. There a senior military figure sat with some interpreters and secretaries around him. With a strong accent, he asked me in my own language for my name, profession and rank in military and working life. One of the people standing around leaned forward and said something so quietly that I could not hear it, but I started when I saw his face. Wasn't that one of my students? I was not completely sure. The chief looked up with an interested expression.

'Aha,' he said, 'you are a research chemist? You have made

an important discovery? Would you like to buy your life with it? Would you like to give us your discovery?'

For a long time afterwards I brooded about why I answered yes. It was not fear. I had been afraid almost all my life, I had been cowardly – what does my book contain except the story of my cowardice? – but just then I was not afraid. All I had room for was an immense disappointment that I would never reach the people who were waiting. Nor did I give any thought to the idea that my life would be something to hold onto under circumstances like these. At that moment, imprisonment and death seemed exactly the same. In both cases my way to the others was severed. When I later realized that it was not my discovery that saved me, that my life would have been spared in any case, that a large number of prisoners meant a desirable gain for the neighbour state as, just as in our State, the birth-rate had not kept pace with the number of casualties in the great wars – it caused me no remorse, changed nothing in my attitude. I gave them my discovery for the simple reason that I wanted it to survive. If Chemistry City No. 4 were to be razed to the ground, if the whole World State were to be turned into a desert of ash and stone, at least I would be able to think that somewhere in other countries and among other people a new Linda would speak like the first one, voluntarily, when some-one tried to force her, and another group of terrified informers would listen to a new Rissen. It was superstition, of course, as nothing can happen twice, but there was nothing else that I could do. It was my only faint chance of being able to carry on where I had been stopped.

How I was later moved to a foreign city, to a foreign prison laboratory to work under surveillance, I have already described.

I have also described how the first years of my imprisonment were full of brooding and anguish. I never managed to obtain any factual information about the fate of the Chemistry City, but gradually I worked out the plan that the enemy had fol-lowed. The intention must have been to fill the streets with gas and prevent any air getting to the lower parts of the city, until the inhabitants in desperation crept up through the few remain-ing exits, one by one or in small groups, and surrendered as prisoners to the enemy's guards. How long the oxygen tanks in the bowels of the city could last and whether the population was brave enough to prefer death to surrender, or vice versa, I did not know. It was also conceivable that the siege failed, that help arrived from other parts of the World State. As I say, I have never been able to find out. But whatever happened, there was a chance that Linda was still alive. Perhaps Rissen, too, if they had not managed to execute him yet. I admit that it is an improbable fantasy, and were I to listen to my common sense I ought surely to spend the rest of my life in despair. As that is not the case, perhaps it merely shows that my instinct for self-preservation compels me to seek comfort in delusion. Before he was sentenced, Rissen himself said: 'I know that what I am is on the way somewhere.' I am not sure what he meant. But sometimes, as I sit on my bunk with my eyes closed, I can see the gleam of the stars and hear the murmur of the wind as I did that night, and I cannot, I cannot eradicate from my soul the illusion that still, in spite of everything, I am taking part in the creation of a new world.

Censor's Postscript

In view of the largely immoral content of the present document, the Censor's Office has decided to add it to the collection of officially declared dangerous manuscripts in the Secret Archive of the Universal State. That it has not been simply destroyed is motivated by the fact that this immoral content may be of use to more trustworthy researchers as material that throws light on the mentality of those beings that inhabit the country adjacent to our own. The prisoner who authored the document and who is still engaged in chemical work under supervision – now with stricter control of the use to which he puts the State's paper and pens – may, in his secretly growing disloyalty, his cowardice and superstition, be a good example of the degeneration that is typical of this inferior neighbour state and can only be explained as a hereditary and incurable contamination that has not yet been fully researched, and from which our nation is fortunately free. If it were to spread across the border, it would be inexorably detected by precisely the drug that the prisoner in question has contributed to manufacturing. I therefore urge those who are in charge of issuing this manuscript on loan to exercise the very greatest caution, and those who read it to subject it to the most rigorous criticism and the strongest reliance on the far better and happier conditions within the Universal State.

Hung Pai Fo
Censor.